How I learned what really (probably) happened to Amelia Earhart

A novel about
the ravishing
Pacific island of Saipan

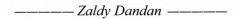

———— Zaldy Dandan ————

How I Learned What Really (Probably)
Happened to Amelia Earhart

Published and distributed by
Padayon Books
P.O. Box 502576
Saipan, MP 969050

This is a work of fiction. Names, characters, businesses, places, events and incidents are either the products of the author's imagination or used in a fictitious manner. Any resemblance to actual persons, living or dead, or actual events is purely coincidental.

Copy editor: James Belyea
Book design by May Phan
Titles and text set in Palatino Linotype, Times New Roman, Baskerville, Old Segoe Script, Narkisim, Elephant, Vinar Hand ITC and Constantia.

ISBN-13: 978-1074076641

For my aunt Merci,
my cousin Abel,
and my sister Carol

Prologue

OF all the things she should think about now, this: she learned that her father was a drunkard when she was old enough to be ashamed about it.

Static on the radio. The humming of the aircraft. Ahead and behind, and all around her, the sea and the clouds: the eternally indifferent, now plainly malignant.

When she saw her father as he lurched home, she ran to her room. Her face was burning with anger. One day, she discovered a bottle of whiskey in his suitcase. He was packing for a trip. She was about to tip the bottle out in the sink when he caught her. Her mother stopped him from slapping his daughter.

Static on the radio. Do they hear me? she thought. Could they? When the fuel finally runs out…what? There's the sea and the middle of somewhere.

He promised to be home by six so he could escort her and her sister to a party organized by the church. The boys she and her sister liked would be there. She and her sister were dressed and ready before 6. But their father came home at 9, drunk and stupidly cheerful. Her sister bawled and ran into their room like fleeing from a burning house.

She was flying into nowhere to be somewhere that had never been anywhere before. During long-distance flights, she had to count the hours to keep track of how much of time she had consumed. No, not wasted. You cannot waste what is inexhaustible. Time is an immensity… On the radio, static. "It's cloudy and overcast," she almost shouted into the radio, hoping that someone could hear her.

Her father brought her to a small dirt strip and paid a substantial amount of money so she could be a passenger on a ten-minute flight. She wore a helmet and goggles and sat in the deep forward cockpit of a big open-cockpit biplane. The pilot was in the rear cockpit. The takeoff was smooth, and soon the plane was up in the air, a thousand feet above Los Angeles and its citrus groves and highways and an occasional ant-like automobile. It was December and the air was cool and clean. As the plane landed dust was everywhere, including on her face, but she was smiling. She liked flying.

"Itasca from Earhart," she barked into the microphone. "Overcast and cloudy, but we're still on course. Will listen on hour and half hour on 3105." Itasca, the United States Coast Guard cutter named after Lake Itasca, source of the Mississippi River. The ship stationed at her destination, Howland Island. Maybe she should whistle, she thought. Maybe they could hear that.

At 63 years old, her father was dying of cancer. He kept asking her about her sister and her mother whom he had divorced six years earlier. So she showed him telegrams that supposedly came from her mother and sister. When he passed away she told her mother, "He was an aristocrat as he went—all the weakness gone with a little boy's brown puzzled eyes...."

"We're running out of gas," she said. And no one hears me, she thought. Or they do but I can't hear them. If something bad happens, they'll probably blame Fred. They say he drinks too much, but he's been a good boy so far. He's probably as exhausted as I am in this cramped, poorly lit navigation area. They'll blame me. She had been awake for more than 24 hours, and flying for, what? over twenty. Stuck in an upright seat which she was unable to leave. What she would give to stretch her limbs. The infernal engine noise, the vibration. The only good thing about all this is when it finally ends. She was tired. She wished she could sleep now. Or take a nap. At least a nap. They'll say she has always been a mediocre pilot. Poor George. Mother.

"We are on the line 157 337," she said. "We will repeat this message. We will repeat this on 6210 kilocycles. Wait."

1

COMMUNISM made me rich. No, not really. This is fiction so I've got to be, more or less, truthful. Let me start again. A Communist triggered a chain of events that improved my livelihood—and brought me *this* close to solving one of the 20th century's most vexing mysteries.

In the early 1990's, I was a police reporter of a newspaper in Metro Manila owned by a greedy businessman. And by greedy I mean someone who, as a young man, had worked hard, had been a daring entrepreneur and a prudent investor. In short, a "good" businessman. They're the worst. They make capitalism work.

So our newspaper union and management were negotiating the renewal of the collective bargaining agreement they had signed a year before. Eventually, management caved in. But our union president, in a sudden fit of Leninist, if not Maoist, indignation, said we should go on strike anyway to teach our capitalist overlord a proletarian lesson. Our leader was short, bespectacled and of medium-build. He had been a student activist at the state university. He was our newspaper's opinion editor. He spoke in multi-syllabic, vowel-sputtering Filipino and wore an army fatigue jacket. He used a scarlet *tubao* (made of native fabric from the tribal south) for a handkerchief and had a native backpack that looked more like a basket or something to catch mudfish with. His heart bled profusely, militantly. He was always dead serious. He also hated the management's negotiating team, specifically the vice president for operations, a condescending, loud-mouthed, boom-voiced English-speaking graduate of an exclusive Jesuit university with a shock of gray unruly hair. Our union leader said we ought, *must*, go on strike. I was quite sure no one agreed with him. I didn't. But no one wanted to contradict him either.

Why? Was it because of the force of his personality? Perhaps. He was a genial man. A good man. He wanted only what was best for everyone, whether we liked it or not. So we were doomed.

If someone had had the balls to point out to him that the strike was pointless, and staging it would be bad for the newspaper, chasing away what few advertisers we had, which would be very bad for us employees, the "debate" would have probably gone along these lines:

UNION MEMBER WITH BALLS: "If we go on strike now it would be like punching someone in the mouth who is handing us a gift."

UNION LEADER: "I submit that your myopic attitude is an authorial simulacrum generated by an ensemble of texts that embodies the multiple historic contradictions of contemporary Philippine society, reproducing these contradictions, inflecting and conjugating them in highly idiosyncratic ways, modifying and altering them, in the same process that the class divisions and the multilayered mode of production—that is, the social relations of production in the total Philippine formation—powerfully shape and overdetermine the ideas, forms, conventions, metaphors, and language structured in the body of texts ascribed to your opinion."

That was entirely lifted from a book by an awesome Harvard-educated Filipino Marxist poet/critic and all-around staggering genius whose works I had tried to read even though they were as enlightening as *Finnegan's Wake* in Swahili *and* Braille.

My point: UNION MEMBER WITH BALLS would have been out-argued. And humiliated. It would have been like going to a gun-fight with, no, not even a knife, but with a used, wet toothpick.

Also, no one wanted to argue with our union leader because several of us had already received phone calls from other newspapers eager to hire us. Most of us no longer cared what would happen to our newspaper. So we agreed to do what most, if not all of us, did not want to do, which was murder, for fun, the newspaper that employed us.

I was sort of sad. And resigned. I had adored *The Daily World* since I was in college. I couldn't believe it actually hired me. Now I was one of the many flabby Roman senators stabbing it after it was already down and bloodied.

2

E went on strike. I slept on the hard, cold floor in the hallway on the ground floor of the newspaper building. I hardly slept at all. After three such nights, I went home, went straight to my room and, soon, had a high fever. My body ached. I was coughing. It seemed like I had the flu. My mother gave me over-the-counter medicines and my fever would subside, only to return. That's right; I was 24 and still lived with my mom. In the Philippines, children will never leave their parents' home unless they're kicked out which rarely happens.

Anyway, after three days, my mother brought me to a specialist whose services I could afford because of the health insurance provided by the company whose existence

I helped end. The doctor examined me and told me to proceed to the x-ray room. Afterward, he stared at the x-ray images of my lungs, looked at me and said, "How the hell did you get pneumonia?" He prescribed a long list of expensive medicines and told me to come back after a week. I was able to afford the medicines because we just received bonuses from the employer we had recently knifed in the back.

After a week of our pointless strike, the newspaper owner announced that he was quitting the biz and informed his former employees to contact the company comptroller, set up an appointment, and get whatever backpay was owed to us.

My pneumonia gone, I started editing news stories for another newspaper, *The Manila Guardian*, but it wasn't the same. It wasn't fun anymore. I didn't know anyone there. I didn't admire the editors. I didn't like the work-schedule. It felt like work.

The Daily World was in Pasig near the then-newly opened huge malls where I watched movies, ate heavenly pasta or bread at The French Baker and browsed through books I couldn't afford to buy. *The Guardian* was in old Manila, near seedy bars, not that I was against them. I missed the *World*, the people I used to work with, our after-work-hour drinking sessions at an eatery near the Rizal provincial Capitol when it was still in Pasig.

One late afternoon, while re-writing yet another horribly written news story at the *Guardian* office, I got a call from my cousin Arnold. He was a playwright by night and an insurance salesman by day. His mother and step-dad had migrated to the states, bequeathing to him their two-story, four-room house in Cubao, Quezon City. The house was near the many nursing schools that were blossoming like clusters of fat flies on an open garbage can, and so he accepted boarders, one of whom was a gay student whose gay lover (but still in the closet) worked for a recruitment agency looking for a reporter.

So I went to the recruiter's office in Ermita near Roxas Boulevard and met the recruiter, George, who looked like one of the Village People—the cowboy but without the hat. He claimed to be impressed with my résumé. Or perhaps he was just in a hurry to recruit someone. In any case, he said: "You got the job." He told me his fee, what documents to get and what tests to take. He said I was to wait for his call. He would go with me to the place where I would be paid in U.S. dollars, six times more than my current pay in Philippine pesos. That place was the island of Saipan. The only thing I knew about Saipan was that it had been the scene of a horrific battle during World War II, and that a nearby island, whose name I couldn't remember, was the staging ground for the planes that nuked Japan. Also it was near Guam. And many Filipinos knew Guam. That's where the Spaniards and, later, the Americans used to dump our "subversives."

I met my recruiter in September. I stupidly quit my job shortly thereafter, only to later learn from him that we wouldn't be leaving until February.

Waiting for my recruiter's call was, quite possibly, the longest, most anxiety-ridden five months of my life. My mother kept asking when I was leaving. She also reminded me about the recruitment fee that my sister, a nurse in Saudi Arabia, had paid in full. My younger brother, an Asian studies (minor in Nippongo) graduate who worked for McDonald's and whose wife was four months pregnant, asked me to find him a job on Saipan.

We were a typical comfortable family because my sister worked abroad. She was in her mid-30's and still single and, as far as I know, never had a boyfriend. Also, once, I saw her French-kissing a girl. I was too confused about what I saw to tell anyone. Although I was pretty sure my mom would freak out. "She's very choosy," my mother would say, referring to my sister. My mother would rather be delusional than disillusioned. My old man, died young, in his mid-40's when I was 13. He was an accountant employed by the city government. He smoked a lot. He didn't drink every day, but when he did, he drank a lot. He also liked "bad" food: deep fried pork and crab fat, in particular. On Christmas Eve, after a day and a night of imbibing, he died in his sleep. It was a cerebral hemorrhage. In death, he seemed to be smiling. Or grimacing.

My mother had been a housewife all her life, but suddenly, she found herself alone and with three kids to raise. At the time, my youngest brother was 11. My sister was 16. With the money she got from my father's death benefits and government pension, mother transformed our small home—which, happily, she and my father owned—into an eatery. Every morning, she got up at 4 to buy meat and produce from the public market. Before 7 a.m., her hot rice porridge with chicken or beef tripe was ready. Mother also sold *sago* and *gulaman*, tapioca pearls and jelly mixed with red food coloring, vanilla flavor, lots of sugar and ice. She had fish crackers and fish balls, candy, banana cue, banana rolls and barbecued pork or beef tripe, chicken heads ("helmet") and feet ("Adidas").

It helped a lot that the public market was just two blocks away from our house in Kamuning when it was still a residential community and not as crowded with stores, restaurants and other commercial establishments that it is now. Among our neighbors were owners of jeepneys and taxi cabs whose drivers were mother's regular customers. And then there was the public school just across from our house and the nearby public health center.

Mother hit the mother lode. A few months after she opened her eatery, she could already hire two helpers— young ladies from the provinces trying to find their luck in the city. More items were added to the menu. She also started lending money, with interest, of course.

My mother, all alone and middle-aged, managed to feed her three children and send them to college.

3

FREAKISHLY bookish teenager, I considered my mother petty-bourgeois. I also took everything for granted and assumed I knew everything. I believed the world had gone to hell in a handbasket, and things had to change for the better. Whether my mother liked it or not. Meanwhile, thanks to my awesome willpower, I resisted taking what I believed was the easy way out, which was to run away, join the Maoist NPA, the New People's Army, or live with the poor in their shanties and enlighten them in the ways of the Revolution. I continued to be fed, clothed and sheltered by my reactionary mother while steeling myself for what I assumed was the coming conflagration. This was in 1985. I was 18, a student at one of the diploma mills in Manila's university belt. I wanted to study at the state university, the hotbed of leftist activism, but my high school guidance counselor, who had to sign my application, noted that, unbeknownst to my mother (whose signatures on my report card I had forged), I wasn't attending my Algebra, Practical Arts and Citizens Army Training classes so how the hell did I expect the state university to actually accept me even if I, by a miracle, managed to pass the entrance examination. I hated my guidance counselor like Stalin hated Trotsky. I couldn't take the entrance examination and, at that point, my mother learned about my truancy. I was lucky I was already taller than she was because she very much wanted to strangle me when she realized that I had been lying through my teeth about my senior year in school.

My mother, God bless her heart, was apolitical. But she cared about good roads, healthcare, public education and public safety. I tried to tell her—I *lectured* her about the Marxian concepts of base and superstructure, surplus value, the semi-feudal and semi-colonial nature of Philippine society, the mode of production, the need for a national democratic phase toward socialism, etc. etc., but she just looked at me like she finally realized she was given the wrong baby after she gave birth in the hospital. To spite me, my mother told me that she would re-name our restaurant New People's Eatery or NPE. (It was called ARB's Eatery, after the first letters of her three children's names: Aurora, Roberto and Benjamin.)

My mother, for the life of her, couldn't figure out why I hated school as much as I liked reading books. Like my sister, she considered reading a chore; something that had to be done like dusting furniture.

I didn't dislike school. I liked English and History and Rizal's novels especially when I learned, no thanks to my teacher, their plots' scandalous underbelly. I loved Human Biology because I could go on and on about Darwin and evolution while my teacher and classmates looked at me like Dante watching the damned souls in the sixth circle of hell. I tried to like Chemistry and Physics but then we had to memorize formulas and do a lot of math. It was like dating a pretty girl who wanted you to accept Jesus as your own personal savior and, worse, after you did that, still wouldn't put out.

I especially loathed Practical Arts which was supposed to teach us basic trade skills like woodworking.

Our teacher, Mr. Fartmouth or something, made us copy lessons from the blackboard, written in clear, feminine script, and they were usually the definitions of terms, like the parts of a hammer, of a saw, of a chisel, the different types of screws and nails and wood and.... I never copied anything. I never listened to him. I read a paperback, usually a Robert Ludlum novel, which I put between the pages of my notebook. And sometimes I pretended that I was writing down all those goddamned words on that dreadful blackboard. And I honestly didn't know why Mr. Buttsniffer or whatever he was called gave me a barely passing grade—until one of my classmates, right after graduation which I didn't attend, told me that my mother had made generous donations to our school.

In college, my brain, or, now I concede, at least the barely functioning parts of it, throbbed with thoughts of Revolution. I read Marx and not just the righteously thunderous *Communist Manifesto*: "You are horrified at our intending to do away with private property. But in your existing society, private property is already done away with for nine-tenths of the population; its existence for the few is solely due to its non-existence in the hands of those nine-tenths."

The *Manifesto*, amazingly, I thought at the time, in the dying days of the Marcos regime, was sold in bookstores. I also managed to get my hands on *Das Kapital*, the massive Penguin paperback. The first chapter, about commodities, fascinated me. Not because it was fascinating, but because I was actually reading it, and the fact that I was doing so, my head swimming in incendiary, illegal abstractions, fascinated me. I was quite sure I was very intelligent. But after the first chapter, all I could recall was a stream of words, like I was watching a bulging, frothing river after a storm, a sight which occasionally— very very occasionally—would yield something of interest like seeing a dog clinging to a log. In *Kapital's* case, it was a footnote regarding the ignorance of the poor, overworked and underpaid workers in Dickensian England, some of whom were quoted as saying: "The devil is a good person. I don't know where he lives." "Christ was a wicked man." "This girl spelt God as dog...." But this spectacle, so to speak, over all, was uniformly, unrelentingly tedious. I stared at a bazillion words. Every single one of them. And perhaps because I had a sado-masochistic bent, I also read *Grundrisse* of which I could remember nothing at all.

Still, Marx was Hemingway, compared to some of Karl's late 20th century progeny:

"This is the moment to re-evoke Bakhtin's idea of intertextuality, the triad of speaker/theme/addressee, as constitutive of the act of communication. Dialectics then instead of functional empiricism. This mode of linguistic comprehension would decenter a self-identical community, foregrounding instead 'the operation of language across lines of social differentiation.' It would focus on modes and zones of contact between dominant and dominated groups and on 'how such speakers [with multiple identities] constitute each other relationally and in difference, how they enact differences in language.' "

My point exactly.

I thought it was my fault for not "getting" Marx. I wasn't ready yet, I told myself. And then I read Lenin's *Materialism and Empirio-Criticism.* I was spellbound. Here was The Truth in blistering prose that I could understand! Such unflagging, unwavering insistence that he, Lenin, was right and that the erroneous philosophical notions he had to critique were peddled by blubbering idiots—it was thrilling for the 18-year-old that I was. Lenin's *Imperialism,* which mentioned the American conquest of the Philippines, was another delight.

Everything, finally, made sense. I had a creed and a mission.

4

HAT I didn't have was money, which I needed so I could be free of my bourgeois wannabe family. I wanted to devote my life to the masses whom I imagined to be very welcoming and loving. I became a member of an above-ground national democratic organization, primarily because it had a small library that had nothing but Marxist books. I joined rallies and seminars and trips to the countryside where we conducted small study groups. EDSA 1986 and the dictator's ouster—these were exhilarating days for me. And because of the new and exciting democratic space that opened up, I wanted to join the Party. I imagined myself working in the city. A cadre immersed in the miseries of the urban poor, organizing them and laying the groundwork for our glorious armed partisans who were making their way from the ever expanding liberated countryside.

I made inquiries about becoming a Party member. I was told by the kindly, soft-spoken chairman of our finance committee that I must wait to be approached. I never was. I would later learn that our finance chairman was a Party member—and, later, one of those accused by the Party of being a deep penetration agent of the government. He "disappeared."

I didn't quit college which turned out to be the smartest thing I've ever done. And my mother, more or less, tolerated my revolutionary fervor. Yet when she learned that I, then in sixth grade, had been talking with the missionaries of the Jehovah's Witnesses, Baptists, Seventh-day Adventists and the Born-Again sects—she was livid. She shooed the heretics away the next time they tried to visit me at our home. She also bought me a Miraculous Medal of the Immaculate Concepcion.

In junior high, I discovered the Indian purple god, Krishna, but this time I hid my copies of Jagad Guru's pamphlets and my new "consciousness" from my mother who would have been horrified.

But she seemed to have considered my activism as none of her concern! Which, come to think of it now, was hurtful. I mean, everyone knew that activists were getting truncheoned, tear-gassed or even shot at. Maybe she believed that my Catholic soul at least was intact so I would go to heaven even if the dictatorship had murdered me.

I was, in any case, glad that she didn't pester me about my political beliefs. My sister considered me a harmless weirdo. My young brother called me a frickin' weirdo, but not to my face because he knew I would have meted out revolutionary justice on his pathetic counter-revolutionary ass. Also, I was still much taller than he was.

I managed to graduate from college. It took me six years to finish a four-year course. I studied journalism. Or mass communications. Whichever. (I'm too lazy right now to look for my diploma.) The most important thing that happened to me in college was that I got to be an intern at that infamous tabloid, *Hoy!* My God that rag printed anything and everything. It had photos of almost naked starlets on the cover *and* on page 3. I loved it. My old editor—I was 18 so everyone over 30 was old—told me to tag along with our police reporter, and I happily did so. In my first month, the sight of the bodies of poor people, stabbed, usually, was shocking. So much primitive, impulsive violence, really, as if it were the easiest, most natural thing to do.

As a Communist, I considered cops fascist puppets of the imperialists' puppets. But they were also nice to me, the cops at the precinct that I covered, regaling me with stories about crimes and criminals and/or dirty cops, which, they assured me, they were not, and of course I said, "Right, of course," as they handed me an occasional copy of the smutty magazines they routinely confiscated from immoral and unlucky street vendors. Sometimes my cop friends even gave me cash, but that's chickenfeed, our old police-beat photographer told me once. He advised me to find a way to get assigned to city hall or Congress or—as he once put it, "I can dream, can't I"—Customs. But that never happened, and after graduation, although I was grateful for *Hoy!* for giving me the proverbial break, I eventually found it embarrassing to be associated with that rag. The last straw was when we ran a story and photo of a middle-aged, mustachioed man sprawled dead in a bed in a room at Joyful Sauna, his tongue sticking out, his privates mercifully covered with white sheet by our photographer before he took the photo. The man had a massive heart attack while being jacked off by the "masseuse" who told me—I wrote the "news" story—that he was groaning a lot during the, um, episode, so she thought that he was totally enjoying it so she, uh, did it faster. That unfortunately exclusive story—MAN DIES HAPPY—appeared on our front page with my byline. It happened on a Saturday evening. Me and a photographer happened to be, well, there at Joyful, too. The police reporters from the other tabloids and newspapers, who didn't appreciate my not sharing the story with them, started calling me Jack. My sister snickered every time she saw me. My brother would just burst out laughing. My mother said she would pray for my soul.

I applied for a job at *The Daily World* and was, oh happy day!, accepted as a correspondent which meant I would be paid per published article based on its length. "Oh so you're 'Jack,' " the old metro editor said to me, grinning. He could have called me Jill and I still would not have minded.

The Daily World! It had the most respected senior editors, columnists and feature writers in the industry. The editor-in-chief was a Harvard lawyer and former cabinet member whose devilish wit informed his editorials which soon became famous or scandalous, depending on which side of a particular controversy you were on. His prose was blunt but moving, elegant but devastating. One of his editorials was titled "Asshole." No lame asterisks to blot out some of the letters. And it referred to the then-chief of staff of the armed forces. "If we cannot have intelligence in government let us at least have good taste," he once wrote. He could write about politics, literature, history, theology, philosophy, movies, showbiz gossip or food with an astonishing level of intelligence. Newspaper readers either adored or despised him. He would arrive at the newspaper office at around 3 p.m., walking hurriedly, while reading a book. With him and carrying his bulging dark brown leather messenger bag with padded shoulder strap was his bodyguard, a six-foot-tall, barrel-chested former Marine we called "Sarge."

I wanted to write like our editor. Of course I couldn't write news stories like they were editorials, and as a police reporter I was still covering the same precinct and basically filing the usual gory stories about weekend drunken homicides, rapes and petty robberies. What I did not do—what I never did—was to beat up "suspects." "Why, are you scared?" our photographer once asked me after he repeatedly kicked an arrested snatcher while taking photos of the snatcher. "No," I replied. "Are you a fag?" the photographer asked me again, looking at me like I was about to French-kiss him. In fairness to our photographer, he was an old man. Probably in his late 30's at that time. Old-fashioned. And by that I mean, an out-and-out reactionary with a "lumpen" mentality.

In my early days as a correspondent, it helped a lot that I became friends with our librarian, Adrian. Part of his job was to measure the printed news stories from correspondents and determine how much we were to be paid. When we became friends, he increased my rate. He did that by adding press releases to the list of my published news stories.

He was a funny man, libidinous and a hard drinker. But whenever he had too much to drink, he would try to beat up anyone who would dare look him in the eye. Like that hapless taxi driver who, of course, was looking at us as we crossed a boulevard at 3 a.m. after a drinking session at one of those squalid, dimly lit bars that had jukeboxes and teenage "receptionists." Adrian saw or believed he saw that the driver was looking at him so he, Adrian, approached the taxi and pounded on the hood while pointing at the driver, who looked old and puny, while demanding that he step out. I managed to drag Adrian away, telling him to have pity on the driver.

But such episodes were rare and never led to an encounter with someone who, unlike us, had a knife or a gun.

5

I WAS still in college when the "bulwarks" of Scientific Socialism in Eastern Europe fell one after the other as their citizens went crazy over MTV and Levi's jeans. Learning that the Ceausescus were crass and corrupt was particularly jarring. The footage of rapturous East Germans rushing to West Berlin on foot was heartbreaking. The following year, the Sandinistas lost the presidential election in Nicaragua. I was inconsolable but never talked about it to anyone, not even to my comrades in our activist group. Gradually, we went our separate ways. Some migrated abroad: to the U.S., Canada or Australia. Others found "respectable" jobs in banking, commerce or academia. One became a very successful entrepreneur. Another had declared himself a vegan and a radical animal-rights activist.

Meanwhile, the Party itself splintered into factions like sects excommunicating each other. I did not want to think about it. My head spun every time I tried to make sense of it all. I was an intellectual orphan, but it felt more like I was abandoned, a wailing infant left outside the door of nihilism. Man does not live by bread alone. But we must have myths, preferably ones that we believe are true and not myths. I realized—despite myself, I had to realize—that my creed, which was supposed to be such a stupendous intellectual achievement, was based on delusions, compared to which religion was more useful and, frankly, more sensible. *That* was shocking.

I remained, or thought I was still a leftist, but of the social-democratic persuasion who wished that the staggering events of 1989-1990 never happened—or happened differently. If life were a vast ocean, my Marxist ideology was my *Titanic*…and it had just hit the iceberg of, what?, Reality? History? Fate? And now I was shivering in the icy Atlantic, clinging to a floating deck chair, swallowing seawater, gagging…

Even as the viability of Revolution continued to diminish before my very eyes, I was starting to enjoy my job at *The Daily World*, particularly after management finally made me a regular employee and a member of the news staff based on the recommendation of our city editor who told our editor-in-chief that my copy needed the least amount of editing, if at all. My secret? Unlike other young or even old reporters who usually submitted their stories by phone or fax (this was the very early 1990's in the Philippines), I wrote mine in our newsroom, first on a typewriter—which I didn't like to use, ever, because revision was messy and required lots of paper and correction liquid and the patience of Mother Teresa. Later, I got to use one of those black Panasonic word processors that looked like a microwave oven and then, finally, a PC that, in those benighted days, had to be booted with a DOS on a floppy disk. It had no mouse. Only Apple's Macintosh had one, and the Mac back then looked like a cute portable TV made by Sanrio.

I wrote in the newsroom and then watched how my editor or his assistant, the deskman, worked on the reporters' stories. I made copies of these edited versions and studied them. I read *The Elements of Style* over and over again. Each week, I clipped the latest William Safire syndicated column, "On Language." I read the works, fiction or not, of writers in English, dead or alive, Filipino or not, who were generally acknowledged to be among the finest: Teddy Locsin *père et fils,* NVM Gonzales, Nick Joaquin, Butch Dalisay, Conrado de Quiros, Edith Tiempo, Ernest Hemingway, George Orwell, Joseph Conrad, Gore Vidal, and even the conservative columnist George F. Will who infuriated and impressed me at the same time.

I wasn't studying; I was learning and it was bliss.

A year after I was hired as a news staffer, our deskman left for a job abroad, Dubai, and so our city editor chose me as his new assistant, and with this new job came a pay raise, not a lot, but still a raise. Of course I liked being a copy editor. My hours were more regular now, and I got to stay in an air-conditioned office. And all around me were the senior editors, my idols.

A year later, we stupidly went on strike.

6

T the time, I was dating Sweet. This wasn't a nickname. It was her name. Sweet Rosales. She was the eldest of three girls. Her sisters were Hope and Holy. Yes one "l"; Holy. Her mother told me that she and her husband took their children's names from one of the prayers of the rosary.

Sweet was a nurse who had just graduated and, as part of her residency, was working for free at a government hospital which also employed my sister. One day, my sister called my mother from the hospital about some documents my sister needed for her overseas job application. I was recruited to take them to her. I saw Sweet at the nurses' station in the hospital's main lobby. She had no make-up. Her face looked so fresh. Her smile glowed. Her almond-shaped eyes were kind and inviting. I cracked a joke. She laughed generously, charmingly. I gave her a call later that same day, and asked her if I could visit her at their house which was a short jeepney-ride away from the hospital. I found her more likeable every time I saw her. I started picking her up from the hospital at the end of her shift, which was 9 p.m., and we would have donuts and coffee at the nearest Dunkin' before we took the jeepney to their home. Her parents liked me. Her sisters too. As one of my gay friends would later tell me, I was one of those guys women would like to bring home to meet their parents. In other words, I looked normal and harmless.

I was also 23 turning 24 while Sweet was 19 turning 20. She wasn't bright. She had to take the college entrance exam twice, and would flunk the nursing board exam twice as well. But I could imagine myself being with her for the rest of my life.

Meanwhile, I was extremely anxious and bored waiting for that call from my recruiter, and enduring my mother's nagging. I should not have quit my job at the *Guardian*. To while my time away I accepted hack jobs, whatever came my way. Advertising copy. Press releases. Term papers. Special advertising features. Speeches. I had to be out there, doing something, thinking of something besides the growing fear that I had been the victim of an illegal recruiter. The embarrassment. Not to mention the recruitment fee that my sister paid and about which my mother would remind me for the rest of my life.

But my recruiter finally did call, in late January, and told me we would be flying to Saipan in the first week of February.

7

HAT followed was the most thrilling week of my life and it included buying a brand new piece of luggage, big and black and with small wheels. And then choosing the clothes—shirts, pants, shorts, shoes—I would bring. For my reading fare, I had acquired cheap paperback editions of *Vanity Fair*, *Tom Sawyer & Huckleberry Finn* (single volume)*, Doctor Zhivago, Don Quixote, Lord of the Flies, The Plays of Aeschylus* (Karl Marx's other favorite dramatist).

Sweet helped me pack. We were together most of the day and night during those seven hectic days, and they were hectic because we wanted to spend a lot of time together. In the evening, she would call from their neighborhood store—this was Metro Manila in the early 1990's when getting a phone for your home took years—and we would blabber like we were high school sweethearts.

We were sad and happy and I was also excited. My flight was to leave Manila at 12 noon on a Saturday, and check-in time was 9 a.m. Two days prior to my departure, I was already packed and ready to go. In the evening, I went out with my friends, Adrian included, of course, and we went to one beerhouse after the other. I got home at past 4 a.m., not minding my mother who was looking at me, shaking her head, frowning, muttering. On Friday, I had lunch and dinner with Sweet. We went to a mall, watched a movie, then headed to a motel before going to their home where I stayed until late in the evening, talking about our plans, which were for me to work on Saipan for a year or two, save money, return to Manila, get splendidly married in church and raise a family in a home we would buy.

On the following day, at 7:30 a.m., I boarded a taxi and told the driver to take me to the airport, which was some 10 miles and a 30-minute drive away without traffic. But in Metro Manila you must include traffic snarls in estimating your travel time, and I did get to airport just before 9 a.m. I was alone. Sweet had phoned me at 6 a.m. She was crying. I was sad but upbeat. She told me to write and, if it was not that expensive, to give her a call at the hospital where she worked. Of course, I said, of course.

My recruiter, George, arrived at the airport shortly after 9 and to while the time away we stayed in the cafeteria where, over coffee, we talked about newspapers and a reporter's work. We boarded our plane just before 12, sitting at the very back, the smoking section. George smoked.

It wasn't my first time on a plane. Back home, I had flown to Baguio and Dumaguete as a roving hack on trips paid for by the company or politicians who needed my services. But those were 45-minute jaunts. The flight to Saipan took three-and-a-half hours, and when we arrived there it was 5:30 p.m., a two-hour difference. It was a pleasant flight. But I couldn't read the book I brought with me, and George was either napping or smoking. I was giddy. I couldn't stop looking out of the porthole. (George wanted to sit near the aisle so he could stand up and light his nth Marlboro if he wanted to.) And all I saw were clouds and the blue sea: 1,633.6 miles of them.

It was cloudy on Saipan, but there was still daylight, and we got through immigration and customs quickly. My first impression: the locals looked like us. They're Austronesians like Filipinos. I would later learn that there were two local groups in the Northern Marianas (of which Saipan is the main island): Chamorros and Carolinians or the Refaluwasch. There were also migrants from the other Micronesian islands: Palau, Chuuk, Kosrae, Pohnpei, Yap, the Marshalls.

The Northern Marianas, like nearby Guam, is American soil and, like Guam, has a significant number of statesiders who are called "haoles," which I learned was originally a pejorative term used by native Hawaiians when referring to Caucasians.

Just outside the automatic sliding doors of the airport was my new employer, Sam Cohen, a former Peace Corps volunteer who had been in the Philippines, Palau, Pohnpei and then Saipan where he met his wife, a local lady belonging to one of the prominent families on island. He arrived in the Pacific in the late 60's when the Northern Marianas and the other islands of the U.N. Trust Territory administered by the U.S were seething with talk of imperialism, self-determination and political status. Like all the young people throughout eternity, Sam said he and his future wife felt that they were at that point in history when everything was about to be upended violently, so it could change for the better, finally, irrevocably; and that they would usher in that stupendous moment, make it happen. Sam and his wife, teachers both, decided to open a newspaper. It was a weekly: an eight-page tabloid-sized, black and white mimeographed publication. It contained island and regional news, opinions, a lot of anonymous letters to the editor and, here and there, small boxes of advertisements for newly arrived grocery items, cars, tires, appliances. As the islands progressed, that rag, *The Marianas Times*, became a twice-a-week, then three-times-a-week and, finally, a five-times-a-week newspaper that, for its New Year edition in the late-1990's, had 136 pages, a lot of them colored.

When the Cohens hired me, the *Times* was the newspaper of note in the Northern Marianas, carrying news from the Associated Press, syndicated editorial cartoons and funny pages while its competitors—surprisingly for a small island, there were six other newspapers—were weekly publications that carried only local stories.

8

S AM was in his late 40s, slim and tall, with thick gray hair. He was from Boston and graduated from Harvard with a degree in comparative literature. Inspired by that suave sex maniac, JFK, Sam joined the Peace Corps and went west—way, way west. His wife, Rosita, was one of the few islanders who, in the 1960s, had managed to get a college degree, an A.B. in English from the University of the Philippines in Diliman. She was in her early 40s, genial, perky and matronly. They had four kids, one after the other, all boys. One was in Seattle, the other in Hawaii; both were in college. The two others were in high school on island.

The newspaper was a family operation. In the beginning, Sam was the publisher, editor and editorial cartoonist while Rosita was the office manager. The reporters were Peace Corps volunteers on island. When the island economy boomed, Sam increasingly focused on the business side of his venture, learning all about the printing presses he and his wife had imported from Manila. He found more ways to expand his newspaper's circulation, including a subscription package that included home delivery, which was not as easy as it sounded even on a small island: most of the roads were unpaved and impassable after a heavy downpour. There were a lot of people who lived on hills, and the streets had no names. The pickup was the vehicle of choice: big tires, four-wheel drive.

When I arrived on island, a Filipino in his early 40s, Manny, was the *Times* editor. There were two other reporters, Filipinos, too, a Bangladeshi photographer, and two editorial assistants: an Indian from Malaysia in her 30s whose husband was a mechanic, and a young Palauan lady.

Our editor, Manny, was tall and already balding and pot-bellied. He seemed either unable to smile or considered it a disability. He had a wife and kid back home, and had been a city editor of the *Manila Guardian* before it hired me. He seemed impressed to learn that I was a deskman at *The Daily World*. In the newsroom, while he was still putting the pages the bed, Manny would speak only occasionally, barking instructions at us now and then. The two reporters were Noel, a former police beat reporter with another Manila tabloid, and Joel, a special advertising feature writer for a Manila broadsheet. Manny had the political beat; Noel was covering the courts and the police; and Joel took care of everything else. With me on board, Manny could focus more on editing and proofreading so we could avoid headlines such as "Governor Fires Ass. Director" or "Pubic Hearing on Breast Cancer." From now on I would cover politics.

Back home, major broadsheet newspapers had a lot of proofreaders on top of several copy and other editors. At the *World*, moreover, a lawyer would drop by just before the pages were sent to the printer. The lawyer's job was to review the headlines and make sure we would not be sued or threatened with a lawsuit on the following day.

The *Times*, in contrast, was a community newspaper. PTA events, graduation ceremonies, school programs, fiestas and the like were our main fare although, of course, we also carried local crime stories and the goings-on at the governor's office and the territorial legislature.

The *Times* had its own building, a two-story structure just across from a sparkling turquoise lagoon and its white sand beaches. It was like looking at a screensaver before there were screensavers. On the ground floor was the reception area and a door that led to the printing presses and the room where newspaper pages were gathered, and copies of the day's edition were bundled and handed to our delivery crew. A short flight of stairs brought you to the second floor and the offices of the publisher as well as the accounting, art, sales and editorial departments. The entire building was air-conditioned, and also on the second floor was a kitchen with a large refrigerator, a toaster, an electric grill, a coffee maker and a microwave oven. Running the kitchen's operation was a middle-aged lady from the Philippines, Nancy, who cooked soups, noodle dishes, spring rolls, rice porridge and pork dumplings. She also sold sandwiches, chips, cookies, crackers, candy and sodas. Her kitchen was open Monday to Friday, 8 to 5. Employees had an open tab and the accounting department made sure we paid each payday, automatically deducting what we owed the kitchen. It was a sweet deal. Eat a lot now, pay much much later.

The nonresident employees—we were also known as alien or, much nicer, guest workers—lived in a housing complex, called barracks, provided by the employer. Ours was located on a hill, a 10-minute drive from our office. It consisted of two white rows of rooms like those found at beach resorts back home. Each had a kitchen, a restroom with a hot shower and a toilet you could flush, and a bedroom with big, screened and curtained windows. It was windy up there and we were surrounded by farm plots that grew tomatoes, eggplant, cucumbers, okra, chili peppers. Our employer's two-story, green house made of stone was nearby. It had a lot of large windows and a big yard.

At our compound, some of the employees had tied hammocks between trees. So my workplace was near a beach, and I lived in what looked like a resort. There was absolutely no pollution of any kind on the island. Compared to Manila's, the streets were litter-free. And there was no rush-hour traffic. Or pedestrians. And I would be paid in dollars, the peso equivalent of which was six times my pay back home, each month. I've just won the lottery, I thought. But I missed Manila.

9

O

N the day of my arrival, my boss, who drove a maroon Toyota pickup, brought me from the airport to a steakhouse for dinner. All the waitresses, including the cashier and the kitchen staff, were Filipinos. Over chit-chat, I ate a huge New York steak, well-done, with peas, mashed potatoes and gravy. I washed them down with two bottles of Budweiser. I had chocolate ice-cream for dessert and two cups of brewed coffee. I could not have afforded such a meal back home. (Unless I were an elected official. Or a convicted criminal about to be lethally injected and was allowed to have a last meal of my choosing.)

At the employee barracks, I was introduced to my co-workers. The women were at a long table just outside the housing units, playing bingo or card games, while the men were having a drink, Miller Lite beer, at another long table. Everyone was cheerful, probably even happy. I joined the drinking session. Everyone wanted to know where I came from back home, which they called the "P.I." How quaint, I thought. I wanted to point out that the last time the old country was called the P.I. was probably just after the war, but I didn't want to sound like a know-it-all jerk. Also, they were asking me so many questions about other things such as the latest showbiz gossip, politics, the economy, traffic on EDSA. After an hour or so of this friendly interrogation, I excused myself as I still had to unpack. They pointed to a room—my unit. The lights were on. Fluorescent. I liked my new home. It was cozy. And the walls were wood: brown and smooth. The wooden floor was polished red. The restroom had a shower, a sink and a toilet, and they were clean and shiny. In my bedroom was a wooden bed with a mattress, a brand new pink pillow still in its plastic case, and a blanket with, like the pillow, a floral design. I also had an electric fan and a clothes cabinet.

As I unpacked, I suddenly remembered that I had not called Sweet yet. I looked at my fake Seiko diver's watch. It was past 9 in the evening already in Manila. (Saipan was two hours ahead.) For sure, someone among my co-workers had a phone. But Sweet's hospital, for sure, wouldn't accept a collect call. (This was the early 1990's; there were no phone cards yet.) I would call her tomorrow, for sure.

I was still unpacking when I heard someone knocking on my door. It was Noel. He was my age, a few months older, and he arrived on island six months ago. He was newly married, and his wife, a nursing student about to graduate, was pregnant and about to give birth.

"Come on, let's go out," he said, looking to his left and then to his right, as if he were a drug pusher.

"Where?"

"Club. Hurry before the *chismosas*, the blabbermouths, notice us."

He had me at "club."

"My money is still in pesos," I said. Thanks to my mother, I had a thousand Philippine pesos which, at that time, was equivalent to $38. (As I write this, 1,000 pesos is worth $18.)

"Pay me back when you can," Noel replied.

He drove a dark brown 1990 Nissan Sentra, automatic transmission, company-owned.

"There's no public transportation here. So I've had to learn how to drive," he said. "You drive?"

"No," I said. In the Philippines, you could live and work, get married, have kids and die of old age without ever learning how to drive.

"It's easy to learn—most cars here are automatic," Noel said. "Like a bump car."

10

THE club, one of many on island, was a five-minute drive away. I would soon learn that "far" on the island meant a 20-minute drive. The club was a one-story building, dark pink, almost house-like, with, like most of the structures on island, a flat roof made of concrete. The sign outside said, "Tokyo Tower."

Like other business establishments on island, the club employees were all Filipinos, except for the bouncer, a hefty, sumo-big dude who was always frowning, and had thick eyebrows, a mustache, and curly black hair.

Noel and I sat near the stage, at the center of which was a stainless steel pole. There also was a bar and a female bartender who, now and then, would throw beer bottles into a large black plastic trash can. The sound of crashing bottles startled me every time it happened. It was all new to me. At the strip bars back home—which, first of all, were usually called beerhouses—the tables were placed far from the stage or at least not too close. The strippers, clad in many layers of sheer clothing, would emerge from a door near the stage which was actually a raised platform on which they would dance, more like swaying really, as if performing a ritual that everyone already knew would not work. The dancers were as indifferent as someone giving a free massage. After peeling off their clothing during the duration of three songs—Bon Jovi, Roxette, Whitney Houston—they get off the stage.

At Tokyo Tower, the first dancer popped out from somewhere behind the stage, like a beach ball. She was an American lady—blonde, tanned, curvy, beaming—and she bounced to the tune of the Pretenders' "Brass in Pocket." This was followed by Free's "All Right Now," and for her finale, the Doors' "L.A. Woman." And oh the things she did with that pole! She climbed, spun and inverted herself as her limbs gripped the shiny metal. And then she would spread her shiny, hairless legs, revealing her shaved womanhood and its pink, rosebud folds.

"I've got to say it's prettier than her," said Noel. At that point I was, for the first time, looking at her face. She was probably in her 30s (but then again, as I would later realize, white Americans usually looked older than they actually were). Her eyes were blue but her lips were thin and her nose was big. She was about to be fat. But by God she was effervescent. And she had so many teeth. Her smile was like a spotlight.

Noel fished out a dollar bill, one of several, from his shirt pocket, waved it at blondie who sashayed toward him.

"This is how you do it," he told me as he slipped the dollar bills one after the other into the dancer's skimpy, shiny golden thong.

"Thanks sweetie," she said smiling like Noel had just swept her off her feet. She blew him a kiss.

The rest of the dancers were Filipino women. Very young. Like newly plucked chicken set free in a yard. Compared to blondie, they were bored and boring, and their music urged us to "listen to your heart" as "there's nothing else you can do," but one of them had bountiful breasts and wasn't unattractive at all and when she saw me, she said, "You're the guy on the plane!" and waved at me like we had known each other since grade school.

We were on the same flight. It was her first night on the job. I liked her smile, I thought, while looking at her mamacitas.

"How much is a lady's drink here?" I asked Noel.

"Seven single, 15 double—and it's in a small glass, Coke, I think."

"So what's the difference between the single and double?"

"A cocktail umbrella. And more ice cubes."

"What's your name?" I asked the dancer as if I was asking her to marry me.

"Come back tomorrow and buy me a drink." And she looked at me the way a man would want to be looked at by a woman he wanted to ravish.

"You don't have an ATM card?" I asked Noel who laughed.

"She's not going anywhere. Not yet. And neither are you."

Noel and I went home just before 2 a.m., which was closing time for the bars on island. When we arrived at the barracks, the bingo/card games and the drinking session had already ended.

"The tattletales are sleeping," Noel said. "See you tomorrow." And he entered the room next to mine.

11

IN bed, in my room, in the darkness, I finally realized that I was far away from home. Neither family nor friends around. Strangers surrounded me. I couldn't sleep. I couldn't even close my eyes. I had two beers early in the evening and a couple more at the club. Normally, I should be dead tired. But no. I was lonely yet excited. I wished I could talk to someone about the day I just had.

I probably fell asleep at dawn and was fully awake at around 7. It was Sunday. There was a cow, somewhere, mooing. I looked out the window. Most of the doors of the other units were still closed. Our barracks were painted white and made of wood with a tin roof. I could live here, I thought, appreciating the private comforts provided by my room. Not home, of course, but homey, in a way.

I went back to my bed. I tried to read a book, but I couldn't. I tried to sleep, but I was restless. I was already looking forward to seeing the island in its full daylight glory. I also wanted a cup of coffee.

I stepped out of my room, wearing blue flip-flops, the big white shirt and a pair of basketball shorts that I brought with me. I was still staring at the bushes near the unpaved road that led to the main road when Noel came out of his room.

"Come on in," he said, referring to his unit. "I've got some coffee. Instant. From the P.I."

Noel was tall, by which I mean taller than me, and I was of average height back home. He was, like most of us at that age, slim. He looked Chinese and was pimply. We talked about our jobs back home, the editors and reporters we both knew. He told me that our editor, Manny, would brief me later that day at the office where we would work on the Monday issue.

"Manny's not here at the barracks?" I asked.

"He lives in an apartment with his wife and kid."

"I thought they were back home?"

"Not that wife and kid."

"Oh."

Noel chuckled as if I just said something stupid.

"And Joel?" I asked.

"He's worse."

"Three wives?"

"Just one, but she's a pastor. They're born-again. They live in another apartment. But no kids, so far."

"When Joel's mad does he say 'Praise the Lord' instead of cussing?" I knew a matron, one of my mother's friends, who was like that.

Noel laughed. "Joel," he said. "What a dork."

As for our Bangladeshi photographer, Malik, he was staying at another compound near our office with other Bangladeshis. He was with his wife and kid whom he brought to Saipan. Malik, like Joel, was slightly older than Noel and I.

"So you can also bring your wife here?" I asked Noel.

"I'm thinking about it," he said. Though it seemed to me he wasn't really.

Manny would later tell me that he was glad I was around so Noel would finally have a friend.

"He mostly keeps to himself and was actually thinking about going home," Manny said.

"So why is he still here?" I asked.

"I asked Malik to teach Noel to drive, and when he did learn, he also learned where the girls are on this island."

I had lunch with Noel in his unit. Fried slices of Spam, fried scrambled eggs with onions, rice from California, Tabasco. I ate a lot while Noel, suddenly, as if for the first time, talked about wanting to go home to be with his pregnant wife, and how lonely he was in the evening, how hard it was to sleep, and how far away his friends and relatives were—how he was always alone day and night. I think I grunted now and then while enjoying my meal. I can't recall if Noel touched his food. But he did wash the dishes which was my cue to return to my room to shower. Noel was already behind the wheel of his company car when I came out of my unit, ready for work.

On the drive to the office, I kept looking at the bright, clear sky as if expecting that it would look different, foreign. On tree-lined Beach Road, the lagoon sparkled.

We were the first ones to arrive at the office. In the editorial room, Noel turned on the air-con and told me where my work station was. All the computers were Macs. The room was neither big nor small, but there were generous spaces in between the desks which were all facing the wall, except for Manny's which was at the end of the room and facing the glass door.

So there I was. About to write my first news story on foreign soil.

"Uh, sir Manny..."

"Call me Manny."

"Manny, sir..."

"Just Manny."

"What will I write about?"

Manny looked at me. I was standing in front of his desk, the largest in the room, on which there were stacks of paper and a phone. He looked bored or sleepy.

"Abi," he said to our Indian editorial assistant from Malaysia. Abirami. "Abi." Her table was near Manny's.

"Yes." She never took her eyes from the Mac as she continued typing. She had big hair, and was dark-skinned, with large dark eyes and a red mole on her forehead that, she would later explain, was not a mole, silly, but a *bindi* which signified that she was a married Hindu woman.

"Give the press release to..."

"Benjie."

"...Benjie."

"Hi Benjie, I'm Abi," she said as she handed me a piece of paper without looking at me.

It was a faxed media release from a university in Hawaii regarding John Cohen's inclusion on the dean's list. He's the publisher's eldest.

"Re-write that," Manny told me. "And, uh, tomorrow you'll go with me to the Hill so I can introduce you to the people there. And advertising also needs you for a supplement." He meant a special advertising feature story.

I didn't say anything.

Manny looked me and said, "We have to be generalists here. But you don't have to help deliver the papers."

Manny first arrived on island in the early 1980s to work for another newspaper, one of those flash-in-the-pan weeklies put out by local politicians. He worked for two of them, one after the other, for two years then went back to Manila, only to return to Saipan a year later, this time to work for the *Times*.

"Here, you'll write a lot of stuff you didn't have to back home. Like sports. Do you know baseball—how to read the stats? American Football, too. And stories about PTA meetings, fiestas, family reunions. Real news stories. Editorials, too, if you want to have my job one of these days."

"Well…"

"I'm not giving it to you by the way. Let's see how good you are first."

"Uh…"

"Our deadline's 5 p.m. Ask Abi here how to format your copy. You know how to use a Mac?"

"Uh…"

"Of course you do."

"Uh…"

"But you have a lot to learn. NMI history, for example. Its constitution. How the government works. The politics. And lesson number 1 is to unlearn what you've learned back home, in terms of covering events and writing news stories."

"Really?"

"I might give you a big story later."
"Okay." I was trying not to sound too eager.
"What do you know about Amelia Earhart?"

12

N

OEL and I were at the office at 9 a.m. the following day, Monday. On the ground floor, in the lobby, people were coming and going, to buy the day's edition, to ask our receptionist, a young local lady, about placing an ad or if they could meet the publisher, the editor or the reporters. On the second floor where the offices were, it seemed that the phones never stopped ringing. Manny was already at his desk, drinking coffee from a black mug, a copy of the day's newspaper spread before him.

"You're going with me," he said. "Governor's office, the Legislature, the Washington rep.'s office."

"Okay."

We rode in his blood-red 1992 Toyota Tercel, stick shift.

"You know how to drive?" he asked.

"Not yet."

"Ask Noel to teach you. His car's automatic."

"Like a bump car."

"Like a bump car." Manny added, "In college, I knocked up my girlfriend."

"Oh."

"We were 19. My old man was furious. He asked one of his friends, a passenger jeepney owner, to let me drive it in the evening and on weekends. So I could at least help pay for the two extra mouths I was bringing home."

"Oh."

"Long story short, I learned to drive professionally."

Outside the two-story governor's office, which was on top of what most people thought was called Capitol Hill—it turned out to be *Capital* Hill—we saw a group of people standing or seated on the steps leading up to a carpeted landing outside the huge glass entrance door.

"Reporters," Manny said. "Flips like us, but one's Palauan, the other two, including the one who looks Chinese, are from the states."

"No locals?"

"Not anymore. Most of them now work for the government. Pays more. Much much more."

Manny introduced me to the other reporters. Most of them said hi. The rest nodded their heads while looking at me. I nodded back, smiling politely. They resumed their discussion.

"They'll do a 902 for the 702."

"What about Compact Impact?"

"CIP's, too."

"That should be included in the 902."

"What did the Wash. rep. say?

I looked at Manny who was smiling; actually, grinning.

"Show offs," he whispered.

We entered the building and in the lobby with its shiny white floor was Jim, the governor's PIO—public information officer—walking toward us. He was from the states, as young as I was. Supposedly a whiz kid. Editor of his college newspaper, worked as a sub-editor for an East Coast city newspaper before joining the campaign team of a Republican candidate for Congress, who won, but then was forced to resign because he was in the closet and was outed by a former lover, a very young black man with a criminal record, and this was in 1992. Someone told Jim about Saipan and he was at that point disenchanted enough about U.S. politics to give island life a try. He joined the cable TV news team and was named PIO by the newly elected governor two years later.

Jim had blue eyes and dirty blonde hair. He wore glasses and was pimply. He looked like he was still in college. He blushed easily. Manny told me that Jim was probably a virgin. And Manny, being Manny, told Jim that he, Manny, believed that Jim had not been laid, ever. "SOB blushed like a virgin redneck," Manny told me. "He's OK." Jim's full name was James Vaughn.

"Vaughn, James Vaughn," he said in his best Sean Connery manner as Manny introduced me to him.

"You're a riot Jim," Manny said with a straight face. Come to think of it, it was the only expression he ever had.

The governor held a press conference every Thursday morning but reporters dropped by every working day to pester Jim. Then they would all go to the nearby legislative building which had many offices and session halls for the Senate and the House of Representatives.

"This is our new reporter for the Hill," Manny told Jim who was beaming at me.

"Are you ready for the big time?" Jim said as we shook hands. His handshake was firm and vigorous. A politician's handshake, I would soon learn. "Glad to meet you."

I never got tired of those phrases: "Good to see you." "Nice to see you." "Glad to see you." Except for our Americanized elite, Filipinos back home never say that to each other. I was flattered that someone told me that he was glad to see me.

"Thanks," I replied.

"I'm guessing your boss has already told you how we conduct the business of the people," Jim said, "and if you still have some questions—ask someone else then." And he laughed.

I smiled. Manny grinned.

"Kidding," Jim said. "Or am I?"

"Anything new?" Manny said it as if he were complaining.

"Lots of good things," Jim said, still smiling as we walked out of the building to join the other reporters who quickly surrounded him. "But you reporters like the bad stuff only, giving all of us the impression that the world is about to end."

"It isn't?" Manny deadpanned.

"Good morning children," Jim said, addressing the other reporters. "I'll fax something later."

"About what?" someone asked.

"You'll see."

"Is it the usual bullshit from you guys?"

"Says someone dripping with it."

Laughter from everyone.

"So can we talk to the governor?"

"Thursday, remember?"

Satisfied that no one among them would get an exclusive story, the reporters, Manny and I included, said goodbye to Jim and proceeded to walk to the nearby legislative building. While everyone chatted with each other, I looked back at the cars in the parking lot outside the administration building, and marveled at the neat rows of brand new SUV's and luxury sedans beside which Manny's Tercel stuck out like a dumpster.

13

L

IKE the governor's office, the legislative building had nothing especially impressive about it. Both apparently were designed to look ordinary and boring but typhoon-proof. Inside, however, decisions that affected the lives of thousands of people were being made. The legislative building had glass doors, and when you entered, you'd be in the lobby, and on one of the walls were framed photos of the incumbent members of the territorial House of Representatives. Another door led to the House chamber, but from the lobby you could already see it through the windows in the wall. You could also hear the proceedings. Each member spoke into a microphone connected to speakers installed in the lobby. The members were seated at a large U-shaped table like the U.N. Security Council's, with the House speaker at the dais, behind which were the CNMI and U.S. flags. Below him was another table where the clerks and the legal counsel sat.

The chamber of the territorial Senate was at the other end of the building. Lawmakers had their own separate offices, with members of the leadership getting bigger ones. The offices of the minority members were near the restrooms.

One of them was Representative Juan Acosta who had a full beard that was already graying. He was in his late 40's, bespectacled, barrel-chested and wore a light-blue, long-sleeved shirt open at the collar, dark blue pants and shiny black dress boots. Manny introduced me to him, and we shook hands. The congressman had a firm grip and looked me in the eye as he smiled like he meant it. "Welcome to the jungle," he said, "we got fun and games." We laughed. Manny didn't get it.

"*Lania* this guy doesn't know Guns N' Roses," the congressman said pointing at Manny. "Rock n' roll!"

Lania/laña/lanya is the all-purpose Chamorro word that could mean "damn," "hell," "crap" or something smellier.

"I don't like music that's too loud congressman," Manny replied.

"*Lania* if it's too loud you're too old!"

I liked Congressman Acosta.

"He's the maverick of the Marianas," Manny said as if it was a disease.

"I'm for the people, that's all," Acosta said.

He was a populist. No one wasn't in local politics, come to think of it, but Acosta alone had the habit of backing the opposition candidate for governor and then later opposing that same person once he was elected governor.

"You've got a new bill congressman?" Manny asked.

"Not yet done *lai* but you guys gonna' love it.*"*

Lai is another Chamorro term that is difficult to translate like *fan* or *nei*, but such words were usually inserted in sentences like "Go there *lai*"; "Check *fan* the coffee"; "Yeah *nei*." More about these later.

"Will it piss off the garment manufacturers?" Manny asked, smiling.

"Hah!" Acosta said.

Saipan had two industries. Tourism and garment manufacturing which was controversial. Garment factories hired foreign workers, mostly Chinese, who sew "Made in the USA" clothing exported to the U.S. for wages much lower than those paid stateside. Garment manufacturers, naturally, were major campaign donors in local politics, and were highly influential.

Acosta hated them because, he said, they liked to buy politicians.

"Shouldn't you also hate politicians who allow themselves to be bought?" I would ask him later.

"*Lania*, I need their and their families' votes."

Acosta, sometimes, was too honest for his own good.

Manny also introduced me to another independent-minded legislator, Senator Leon Guzman. Like Acosta, he was middle-aged, but short and round with curly graying hair, and he always wore suspenders. A minority bloc member, he liked to take swipes at the leadership during sessions.

"Those guys need to be reminded that they won't be calling the shots forever," he said, referring to the majority bloc. "So when we finally kick them out they won't be crying too hard." And he laughed as if this had already happened.

Our next stop was the copy room manned by a wiry Palauan man named Johnny. He had red teeth, fierce face and an easy, reassuring smile. On one of the walls in this room were cubby holes marked with the names of the lawmakers and the media outfits. There were also two huge state-of-the-art copying machines and a long table on which there were stacks of documents.

"This is the most important person in this building," Manny said as he introduced me to Johnny who chuckled.

"So you have a new victim huh," he said.

"Shhh; don't tell him," Manny said and they both laughed.

"If you need copies of any documents, Johnny's the man," Manny told me as he handed Johnny a copy of the day's *Times*.

"Thank you thank you," Johnny said as he, in turn, handed Manny the documents in the *Times'* cubbyhole.

"And be careful with the paper they use here," Manny told me as he looked at the documents. "This is real paper. They can cause cuts which hurt like hell. It's not the onionskin crap we use back home."

We walked back to the governor's office "just in case," Manny said. Just in case the governor was there. Lo and behold, he was. He was about to get into his black Lincoln Town Car, big and glossy.

"Governor!" Manny said. We walked quickly to the tallest man I'd seen so far that day. He was smiling like we just caught him with his hand in the cookie jar. He held onto the open door of his car but didn't get in.

"*Lania* I thought I was getting away scot-free." Edward Gutierrez Sanchez, who convincingly defeated the then-incumbent governor in the last elections, stood six feet tall. Of medium built, he had a receding hairline, gray at the temples. He also had gray curly hair on his forearms. He was wearing a Hawaiian shirt, the color of wine with red-veined big blue leaves, and Dockers khakis. His big brown leather shoes looked battered but newly shined.

"You better talk to Jim," he told us, referring to his spokesman.

"I just want to introduce you to our new reporter, Benjie," Manny said as I extended my hand to the governor who grabbed and pumped it.

"Nice to meet you *lai*," he said looking, it seemed, deep into my eyes. "If this guy," meaning Manny, "doesn't treat you well, just tell me OK." And he laughed. "I gotta' go."

As we watched the governor's car pull out of the parking lot, Manny said, "I was told he knows something about Amelia Earhart."

14

MANNY treated me to lunch at D' Exquisite, owned by a Filipino couple who had been on island since the very early 1970's. They had been cooks and/or kitchen helpers at Saipan's first hotel. They met and got married on island. They were among the few nonresidents who were granted permanent residency by the territorial government. Their restaurant was, by now, one of the oldest on Saipan, and was a favorite among locals and Filipinos.

D' Exquisite (it's a Filipino thing; using D' instead of "the") was like a cafeteria—a clean, air-conditioned, not-of-the-Third-World cafeteria. The dishes were in stainless steel trays in glass display cases that kept the food warm. You get a generous serving of California rice and two choices of food and bottomless iced-tea. Prices were very reasonable.

"Small far-away island in the middle of the ocean," Manny said as we dug into our fried chicken and bowls of vegetable stew. "Back in the day there were only fish and sweet potatoes here, but then they planted the American flag, and suddenly there was plenty of good, affordable food for everyone. You better watch out though," he told me. "You'll balloon up in a year." And he patted his tummy.

Back at the office, Manny told me to write about some of the recently introduced resolutions and bills we got from the Legislature while our editorial assistant Abi taught me how to format my news stories, how to print them, and how our network system worked so I could just place the electronic copies of my stories in the designated folder on my Mac desktop.

"As I've said, you now have to forget everything you've learned about news coverage in Manila," Manny said.

I looked at him.

"Have you read Karnow's *In Our Image?*"

I shook my head.

"He said Philippine journalism seems to be stuck in the 1930s. Here they won't let you forget that." He paused. "And we're considered pests, rarely useful, usually just annoying. Back home we're pampered by the powers-that-be. Here we're just nosy foreigners who can't write good English and have absolutely no idea what journalism is."

"Really?"

"Who is Noel!" A middle-aged man coming up the stairs to the second floor was shouting. We could hear his rubber flip-flops slapping the floor which was covered with yellow linoleum. He pushed open the glass door to the editorial office, looked at us as if he had just caught us cheating with his wife and said, "Who the hell is Noel!" He wasn't asking a question. He was shouting an order.

"May I help you?" Manny was firm.

"Are you Noel!" He still wasn't asking.

"I'm his editor."

"*Lania lai!* Why you do that!"

"What did we do?"

"*Si* Noel, today's news!" And he was waving a copy of the day's paper at us like a magic wand that would turn us into toads.

Manny just stared at the man who then pointed at a news story on page 3. The headline read: "Teen Arrested for Theft."

"That's my son!" the man said.

"Were we wrong? Your son didn't steal anything?"

"Why do you have to write about it!"

"It's from the police report and—"

"You don't care because you're not from here!"

"We're just doing our job—"

The man started speaking in Chamorro.

Enter our publisher, looking bored.

"Hello fellows," he said, looking at the angry local man who grumbled, "*Lania* Sam!"

"Good to see you, too, Ray."

The local man spoke in rapid Chamorro, pointing, once again, at a news story in the *Times*.

"Okay, okay, I'm sorry to hear that," Sam replied. "Let's go to my office and talk about it over coffee—decaf for you."

The local man was shaking his head, but he followed Sam who stepped out of the newsroom and entered his office.

"The boss speaks local?" I asked Manny who hadn't gotten up from his seat and was again typing on his Mac keyboard like nothing had happened.

"He understands it, but can't really speak it."

Pause.

"So what was that about?" I asked.

"Reader feedback."

"Does that happen a lot?"

Manny looked at his wristwatch. "Well, the day's long. And it's either they come here to complain or call me or the reporter, scream at us and threaten a lawsuit."

Pause.

"As I've said, it's different here," Manny said. "Any person you mention in a story—they react immediately, and in your face. Wrong spelling of the name or place. Misquotation. The headline. The way you 'angled' the story. The placement of the news story. Or just because you wrote about them."

"Man," I said.

"I kindda like it, sort of," Manny said. "At first I hated it, but then I decided to consider it a challenge, you know, to do better. But that's still not a guarantee that no one will complain. Especially with police stories about domestic cases."

Pause.

"I should have listened to my old man," Manny said. "He wanted me to be a seaman." He chuckled. "I could have been scraping rust now on a ship headed to Greece."

Manny's phone rang. "Hello? OK." He looked at me. "Sam wants to talk to you."

"Am I in trouble?"

"Not yet I think."

15

SAM was at his executive desk, reading the day's *Times*. He sat in a black, modern-looking executive chair. Behind him was a walnut TV stand on which were arranged several small framed photos of him and the mrs. and their children. In the two glass-front cabinets were books, and there were more books where the VCR should be. On the wall behind him were framed certificates or plaques of appreciation from government agencies and community organizations, including the chamber of commerce and the Rotary Club. There was an L-shaped sofa against the wall near the door and two desk chairs, no wheels and no arms, placed sideways in front of his desk.

"Hi Benjie take a seat," Sam said as he put the newspaper on his desk. He was looking at me like it was the first time he had ever seen me.

"So how's your first day so far?" he asked.

"Exciting." I smiled.

"Yeah, that. We get a lot of that but only because, and I'm not bragging, this newspaper matters in the community. What we publish is read by ordinary people, business leaders, politicians, government officials. We set the tone of public discourse. You know why?"

"No sir."

"Our competitors are owned either by politicians or businessmen. Now I've got nothing against them, competition is good and all that, but that's the reason, whether they like it or not, they have to read our paper. They know we have no ties to politicians or special interests. But of course that's also the reason the powers-that-be don't like us—well, they do, when they're still in the opposition. When they're in power then we end up 'irritating' them as much as we did the previous leadership. That's how it is."

I was still smiling.

"If you want people to like you, then you're in the wrong job." Sam chuckled. "So you'll cover the Hill, and maybe write an editorial or two each week?"

"Yes sir."

"Manny writes one editorial a week, for our Friday issue, and now that he won't be covering any beats, I've asked him to write for Monday and Wednesday, too. I know it's not easy to write editorials, and I really want him minding the store here while I go out there and get us some business."

"OK sir."

"OK then. Now if you get angry calls or if someone angry wants to talk to you about what you wrote make sure you tell them to come talk to me instead."

I nodded.

"What about your room at the barracks—is it OK?"

"Oh yes sir."

"I know it's not the Hyatt, but I made sure it's comfortable and everyone has privacy."

I nodded.

"We make our drinking water, so you don't need to buy."

I was still nodding.

"We're on an island in the middle of the Pacific and the groundwater is salty. But there are water companies that sell drinking water, and I decided to make my own, considering I've got a lot of employees."

I nodded.

"I must be boring the hell of you."

"No sir." I was bored. I almost nodded.

"They call you cheap labor, do you know that."

"Oh."

"And the people who usually say so are those who can't even afford to hire one worker." He chuckled. He sounded as if he was rehashing an old argument.

"Anyway, for the rest of the week, you go to the Hill with Manny, and if you've any questions just holler."

"Yes sir."

"By the way, what do you know about Amelia Earhart?"

16

I N the editorial room, it seemed that Manny's main job was to answer the phone. Our editorial assistants, Abi and the young Palauan lady Connie, who was on duty on weekdays only, had phones on their desks, and they were always ringing. It was one phone call after another. Complaints. Thank-you's. News tips. Complaints. And most of them were for the editor. Or to the reporters Noel or Joel who arrived from their beats one after the other later in the afternoon.

Joel was a bit older than Noel and I. And he often dressed as if he were going to church for a Christening ceremony. Tucked-in, buttoned-down, short-sleeved shirt with a patch pocket. Dark blue pants. Black leather shoes. His hair was always neatly trimmed and parted at the side. He talked as if he wanted to sound like a radio announcer. He liked "clean" jokes and never joined Manny and Noel when they talked about women—i.e., bar girls. And Joel would just smile whenever Manny would rib him about God and the Holy Spirit.

But it was quiet for most of the afternoon and early evening as everyone had to transcribe interviews and write the four stories required of each reporter while the editorial assistants typed the press releases or letters to the editor faxed to our office. Manny laid out the pages on dummy sheets which, when done, would be handed to one of his two assistants who would bring them to the art room, which was next door. There, several graphic artists worked on their Macs, creating advertisements for our clients or the pages of the next day's *Times*. Once they were printed, they'd bring them to Manny for proofreading. Thursday, I would soon learn, was the busiest day of the week. That's the day when we had to work on the Friday edition which usually had 44 or 48 pages—or more. Before the economy took a nose dive following the Asian currency crisis in the late 1990's, our end-of-the-year Friday edition had 136 pages which we finished printing late Friday afternoon.

Reporters who had already met the "quota" helped proofread some of the pages especially on a Thursday evening. The hours could be long. It was never a 9 to 5 job on weekdays. It depended on the events of the day. And the pay wasn't high. On Saipan it was way higher than in the Philippines, sure, but compared to what other jobs paid— nursing, for example, or civil engineering—a reporter's salary was peanuts. So why be a journalist? I guess I wanted, somehow, to change the world for the better, and I wanted to write literature which I believed could also change the world for the better. Ah yes; the conceit of a young nerd. And I was pretty sure that a stint in journalism would help me write better and learn about real life. Also, in the P.I., journalism, like the law, medicine or teaching, was a respected occupation. There was some "prestige" attached to it. We're a Third World country that was a colony for almost 400 years. We value and look up to "intelligent," educated people, those who use their minds to perform their work. Manual labor was for the unlucky.

When I was a child, my playmates in the streets included children who were from poor families. And sometimes we would talk, and they would ask me if my family was rich, and I would tell them I didn't think so. And one of them said, but you're not poor. And I said, I believe we're not. And he said, we're poor—and they were: their daily diet was usually rice and salt; that's it. We're really poor, he added, so when I grow up I want to work in an office. What office? I asked. Doesn't matter; it just has to be an office, and I will wear shoes, and pants and a long-sleeved shirt, and maybe a tie, and there will be a typewriter in front of me, and I will flirt with the boss's pretty secretary.

Until the movie *Revenge of the Nerds* was shown in Manila two years after it was released in the U.S., I wasn't aware that nerds existed. In my high school the jocks and the smart-set were one and the same. They were into books and sports and the other sex, and not always in that order.

Anyway, journalism back home was a highly regarded occupation. Imagine my surprise when I learned that in the U.S., journalists were ranked with lawyers and politicians as the most mistrusted if not despised professions. On Saipan, where most of us were foreigners, we were not exactly adored either.

17

I
N the Philippines, the powers-that-be consider reporters accomplices. We reporters are thrilled by our proximity to government officials and happy for the crumbs, small and big ones, thrown our way. Eventually we come to assume we're as important as the famous people who call us by our first names, and remember us on our birthdays and on Christmas.

On Saipan, we're basically treated like a mild case of eczema that flares up now and then, irritating but tolerable. But because the island is American territory, many readers expect that their tabloid-sized, five-times-a-week newspaper with one editor and three reporters whose English is a second language should produce journalism that, at the very least, is comparable to what is published by major U.S. dailies.

Fine. However, most Filipino journalists believe that news stories must be sensational—that facts should be interesting even if they're not. We seldom inform; but we always try to entertain. And we're into he-said-she-said reporting, often in two parts. He-said today; she-said tomorrow. "In-depth reporting" means having a paragraph or two of "background information" that is usually based on hearsay or unverified. Sometimes we interview our fellow reporters or ourselves and cite them as "sources." The U.S. has investigative reporting. We have what the Marcosian Martial Law regime called developmental journalism which is also known as envelopmental (cash in an envelope) reporting.

To be sure, based on the law of averages, not all Filipino journalists are inept or corrupt. Many, myself included, believe in our profession's mission which we're quite sure is noble, uplifting, heroic and glamorous. Many of us thought that Joe Burgos, the incorruptible newspaper publisher who defied the Marcos dictatorship, was the rule and not, as it turned out, the exception.

As a Filipino journalist on Saipan, you realize all this—but only after years of getting scolded by statesiders who are appalled, as our publisher Sam would put it, that the island's leading daily is not exactly like *The New York Times*. No one seemed to be aware of the high costs of running major publications which have legions of staff and editors, including lawyers.

And then there were our typos. Right after Sam had a big falling out with his stateside editor (another Peace Corps volunteer), no one was really proofreading our newspaper *before* publication. But once it's printed, everyone's an editor. "Pubic hearing." Wrong dates. Wrong spelling of names. Wrong names. Wrong photos. Wrong captions. A Toyota hatchback became a Toyota hunchback. "Bad advice" was turned, God knows how, into "butterflies." There was this story quoting an unnamed "source," who was a lawmaker but whose picture was included in the story. Sam said the news story should have stated: "According to our source who declined to be identified but quite happy to be photographed…."

I don't know if it was middle-age or Zen Buddhism, which he said he found sensible, but by the time I worked for him Sam was a picture of serenity. His specialty was handling irate officials and/or readers. As for our "bloopers," he would gently point them out to us then tell us how we might avoid them next time. ("Read the headline backwards, word for word.") Sometimes, he was the first to laugh at our mistakes, to treat them like wholesome jokes. What, for example, should have been "there is no hope in dope" in a feature story about drug rehabilitation came out as "there is no hope in hope." Sam laughed out loud. "We have Schopenhauer in the house!" he said. "Who's that?" Joel asked Manny. "Someone who hated your God," our editor replied.

Many years later, I would learn that in Britain, newspapers would rather *not* correct their factual errors unless they have to. And when they do, they do it with great style:

"The great crested newt shown on the front page of the Society section…was, as sober inspection confirms, upside down."

"Yesterday was Wednesday, despite an assertion that it was once again Tuesday."

Compare these with the corrections published by some U.S. newspapers:

"An April 5 story stated that Mary Fraijo did not return a reporter's calls seeking comment. Fraijo died last December."

"Due to a typing error, Saturday's story on local artist Jon Henninger mistakenly reported that Henniger's band mate Eric Lyday was on drugs. The story should have read that Lyday was on drums."

The Brits would have come up with something witty like what the American novelist Ann Patchett wrote in a letter to a U.S. publication:

"I was grateful to see my book *This is the Story of a Happy Marriage* mentioned in Paperback Row (Oct. 19).

"When highlighting a few of the essays in the collection, the review mentions topics ranging from 'her stabilizing second marriage to her beloved dog' without benefit of comma, thus giving the impression that Sparky and I are hitched.

"While my love for my dog is deep, he married a dog named Maggie at Parnassus Books last summer as part of a successful fund-raiser for the Nashville Humane Association.

"I am married to Karl Van Devender. We are all very happy in our respective unions."

18

ON Saipan, there were people who believed—who were pretty sure—that Amelia Earhart died on their island which before World War II was Japanese territory like the other Micronesian islands except Guam. Apparently, so the story goes, she was spying for the U.S. government during her famous final flight in the summer of 1937 that resulted in her and her navigator Fred Noonan's disappearance.

I was told that local eyewitnesses saw Earhart and Noonan both of whom were locked up in the Japanese jail on Saipan. (Today, what remains of the jail can be seen on Middle Road, one of the island's main thoroughfares, near some private homes, an auto-shop and a former gay bar.)

I was told that "it was common knowledge" that Earhart and Noonan died and were buried on island. Some old villagers said they could point out the spot where Earhart and Noonan were buried.

Certain American Marines who landed on Saipan during the war would swear that they found Earhart's briefcase containing her passport and visas, and that they saw a silver, single-wing, twin-engine airplane matching the description of her Elektra in a hangar on Saipan in 1944. They were ordered to destroy it by an "insistent" "man-in-a-suit" who also told them to "never tell anyone" what they saw. The Marines, so the story goes, "climbed onto the plane and poured three or four five-gallon cans of gasoline all over it. Then a P-38 flew over it and fired tracers at it from behind, causing 'humongous fire and smoke.' "

Here's another story that I would learn from locals:

In Nov. 1977, four Chamorro women were interviewed on Saipan by a Catholic priest, and they talked about what they said they witnessed in the late 1930s.

One of them said that sometime around 1937, she saw "a foreign woman, thin in stature with brown hair, cut short similar to that of a man [who] would sometimes pass her house and on one occasion, looked 'sickly' with one side of her body and one hand burned. The foreign woman, with whom the Chamorro lady could not communicate as she did not speak English at the time, was believed to be staying in a nearby building referred to by the local people as a hotel. This woman gave a ring with a 'white' stone in it along with some pleasant smelling balsam to the young Chamorro girl. Later, two Chamorro girls were asked to make two wreaths and, when asked why, the girls were told that the 'American' had died of 'amoeba' (dysentery or diarrhea). The Chamorro woman related that when the foreign woman was alive she was guarded. The other Chamorro woman recalled that as a child she remembered hearing that a plane had crashed 'southwest of us' and the pilot was a woman. The Chamorro said the Japanese were 'very startled' because she was piloting the plane. Still another Chamorro woman stated, 'it could be 1939 or something like that when I first heard there was a woman spy who came to Saipan but they said she was most likely killed. But I did hear that an American woman was caught spying.' Another Chamorro woman when interviewed recalled 'hearing about a plane that crashed, the topic of conversation in Saipan. I remembered going to church. I wanted to light a candle for my husband because a battleship was scheduled to come into port about 10 o'clock in the morning. The plane was exhibited and that was when the Japanese made an announcement to all the people that those who wanted to see an airplane may come and see it. That was the year 1937 or 1938. There was talk about the plane having fallen down in the island south of us in Micronesia. I know of a ring that belonged to that woman. I don't know what ever happened to it."

A great story. As I write this, however, no one can either prove or disprove it.

Here's what we do know (my source is Erik Shilling of *Atlas Obscura*):

"On July 2, 1937, [Earhart] and her navigator, Fred Noonan, disappeared while flying in a Lockheed Model 10 Electra in the South Pacific. They were aiming for Howland Island, about 2,000 miles away from their next destination, Hawaii, and about 4,500 miles short of their ultimate destination, Oakland, California, which would have completed Earhart's round-the-world trip. But the two never made it. Earhart's last radio message said that 'we are on the line 157 337'—157 degrees to 337 degrees—and 'we are running on line north and south.' Or maybe she said 'north to south.' Or 'north then south.' Or something else entirely. But then came nothing.

"The U.S. Navy looked for a few weeks and came up empty-handed, deciding ultimately that Earhart and Noonan crashed and sank into the Pacific Ocean. But almost immediately, there were whispers of conspiracy. This was in part because of brewing tension in East Asia, where Japan and China had already clashed over Japanese incursions into Manchuria. Within a few months of the disappearance, an Australian tabloid reported what it said was the real reason Earhart vanished: to give the U.S. an excuse to search for Japanese military installations."

19

MY publisher and editor said they knew someone who had evidence indicating that Amelia was on Saipan. Let me rephrase that. They said they knew someone who knew someone who might have proof. But they didn't know what that was. So they wanted me to work on the story.

"Just imagine," Sam said to me. "More people would be interested in this island. History buffs from the states! They'd be all over the place!" News about Saipan had been mostly about labor abuses involving alien workers. "So tacky. We need to change our image," Sam said.

So who was our "source"? I asked Manny. Who was the dude who knew the dude who might know something?

"He's an old local guy," Manny said.

"Likes to drink," Sam said.

"A lot," Manny said.

I chuckled.

"But he knows something, I was told," Sam said.

"And he doesn't want to talk about it when he's drinking or drunk already," Manny said.

"Our problem is, he's seldom sober," Sam said.

"So how do we know he knows what he knows," I asked.

"Other local people say they hear that he knows," Sam replied.

"Do other reporters know about this?" I asked.

"If they do, they're not saying," Manny said.

So where do I come in?

"You've got to find him," Sam said.

"And then you've to talk to him," Manny said. He and Sam learned about this guy recently, and they wanted a reporter assigned to the story. And that's where I, newly arrived, came in.

"We don't want to spook him," Sam said.

"Don't spook him," Manny said.

His name was Jose Gomez. A widower in his 60s. His two daughters were married and had families of their own and were residing in Oregon. He didn't have a lot of other immediate relatives on island. He lived somewhere in Chalan Kanoa which used to be known as the "capital" of Saipan.

After the war, most of the locals lived in CK, located in the southwest of the island, Sam said. But many of them moved to the homestead villages up north or further down south as the local economy came alive in the 1980's.

Where can I find Jose Gomez?

"Check out the bars in CK," Sam said. "Ask around. But again, don't push it."

Why not approach people we know who know Jose?

"I don't know anyone who does, which is quite strange, I know," Sam said. "And right now, everything's hearsay. But maybe you can learn who these folks are who know Jose."

Manny would later tell me: "Sam wants to see if he can count on you so don't blow it."

Okay. So where to start?

Manny said he would take me to the bars in the CK area that night. There weren't a lot of them."

"Tokyo Tower?" I asked, smiling in my mind.

"Yeah that's one of them." Manny looked at me.

I was smiling.

20

IF you're from the Philippines, you can think of Saipan as being smaller than Quezon City, but slightly larger than Manila, Makati, Pasay, Malabon and San Juan combined. If you're from the U.S., Saipan is slightly larger than the Bronx.

As for the island's history, for many residents it consists of what they remember; what they've heard from other people; or what they can Google. There are books that deal with specific periods of the island's history and a more or less comprehensive textbook that covers the pre-Spanish era and narrates events up to 2015. But talking to people about Saipan's history reminded me of the story about the blind men who tried to describe an elephant after they touched it.

"It's a pillar," said the blind man who touched the elephant's leg.

"No! It's like a rope," said the other blind man who touched the tail.

"No! It is like a thick branch of a tree," said another blind man who touched the animal's trunk.

And so on.

For many, Saipan was a major battlefield in the Pacific theater of World War II. Nearby Tinian was where the *Enola Gay* and *Bockscar* took off to nuke Hiroshima and Nagasaki.

When Saipan's economy boomed in the 1980's it became notorious among U.S. media outlets as an "island of slaves," where abuses committed against alien workers were "rampant." "Shame on U.S. Soil," as one American publication would put it.

For tourists, who were mostly Japanese, Saipan was the tropical pleasure island: white-sand beaches, all-year-round sunny weather (if there are no typhoons, that is), smiling, hospitable native people, a shared history, the American flag.

For foreign workers like me, it was a land of opportunity where we could earn and save U.S. dollars, thank you very much foreign exchange rates. It was also a place where one could try new things, meet new people, learn about new cultures.

For locals, it was home, of course. And for many of them, it was irksome to see that home inundated by foreigners from the Third World as well as pontificating, scolding, on-a-mission-to-save-the-world-one-island-at-a-time statesiders.

Among statesiders, many came here to "try something new"—to get away from it all in a faraway place where there's no winter (just typhoons), and where one can go scuba diving, parasailing, spelunking, hiking or camping out on the beaches. Where things were "exotic" but remained comfortable with the assuring presence of the American flag flying above it all.

Local history for many of us began when we arrived on island. What happened before the islands became a U.S. commonwealth in Jan. 1978? There was the Trust Territory government administered by the U.S. on behalf of the United Nations. And before that: the Battle of Saipan, the Japanese administration, the short-lived German administration, and a long period of Spanish colonial rule. What exactly happened during those historical periods was anyone's guess if anyone cared to think about it at all.

21

FTER he put all the pages to bed, Manny and I grabbed a quick bite at D' Exquisite and headed to Tokyo Tower. Clubs on island usually opened at around 7 p.m. We arrived at 8. It was a weekday, and there weren't a lot of people there yet. The girl I met earlier was "tabled" by a middle-aged man who looked Filipino. They were laughing. Oh my heart, my beating heart!

Manny said, "I just realized how ridiculous it is to assume that we can just enter a dark, noisy place of sin, as Joel would put it, and ask strangers—horny drunks at that—if they could help us find another stranger."

I chuckled.

"Let's just sit back and look around," Manny said.

So we watched bored Filipina dancers swaying and writhing while we looked, now and then, at the other patrons who were ogling the naked women on stage. No stateside dancer that night. I learned from one of the waitresses, who were all Filipinas, that the stateside dancers were based on Guam, but they would perform on Saipan now and then. Meanwhile, Manny was hoping to see a familiar face in the dark which was barely lit by the colored lights on stage.

"Do you know the bouncer?" he asked me.

"It's only my second time here," I replied.

"What about that guy?" he asked me, looking at the direction of a middle-aged, local-looking man with a big beer belly who was the only customer at the bar.

"I don't know him," I said.

"I think I do," Manny said as he stood up and walked to the bar. They did know each other, and I watched as they shook hands and exchanged pleasantries. Then Manny flashed the "V" sign at the Filipina bartender who gave him and his friend two bottles of Budweiser. They talked, Manny and the local man. Eventually, Manny looked at me, and nodded. So I went over to them.

"This is our new reporter Benjie," he told the man who offered his hand which I shook.

"Pete," the man said.

"He used to work for the governor's office," Manny said.

"Retired?" I asked.

"No *lai*; just waiting for my party to get back in power."

We talked. Or tried to, over the loud music and the gibberish spouted by the Filipino DJ, trying his best to sound like a radio announcer with a baritone voice, as he introduced each dancer.

Pete had heard about the Amelia Earhart story, and about the local man who might know the other local man who knew something.

"I think that's old man Joaquin, *Tun* Jack."

Tun and *tan* are Chamorro terms of respect for an elderly man and woman.

"You sure?" Manny asked.

"Or maybe he knows the one," Pete said.

"Where can we find him," Manny asked.

Pete told the bartender to give him another bottle of Bud. "These guys are paying," he said, pointing to us. "But when I get my job back," he told Manny, "beers on me." He took a swig from his bottle. "He'll be here in a few."

"Really?" I had to ask.

"It's your lucky night," Pete said. And lo and behold, there was *Tun* Jack, taking the stool next to Pete. They spoke in Chamorro, then Pete introduced us to the old man. *Tun* Jack. He smiled when Manny asked him about Amelia Earhart.

"*Matai* already," *Tun* Jack said, looking at his bottle of beer.

"Who's dead sir?" Manny asked.

Tun Jack and Pete spoke in Chamorro.

"The man you're looking for passed away just recently," Pete told us.

"But what he knew I know," *Tun* Jack said. He and Pete spoke in Chamorro again.

"I know," *Tun* Jack said.

"Can you tell us?" Manny asked.

"Why not," *Tun* Jack said. "But not tonight. Pete," he said to the other local man, "tell us that joke about the plane."

Pete chuckled and said: "There was this small plane flying somewhere in the Pacific, and it had four passengers: one Chamorro, one Japanese, one Americano and one Filipino. Then the plane started having engine problems. So the pilot told his passengers to throw away some of the things they'd brought with them so the plane would not lose altitude. And so the Japanese threw away his laptop and other electronic gadgets and said, 'I've got a lot of that anyway back home.' Then the Americano threw away his stash of marijuana and pills and bottles of whiskey and said, 'I still have a lot of those back home.' But before the Filipino could throw away anything, the Chamorro grabbed him and threw him out of the plane. 'Plenty Filipinos back home.' "

Manny and I laughed out loud—beer actually came out of my nose.

22

T

HIS was not like driving a bump car, I told myself. I was behind the wheel of Noel's company-issued, Nissan Sentra and we were on the former airfield in As Lito, in the southern part of the island. What used to be a runway was now a place where newly arrived foreign workers could learn how to drive.

"I should have enrolled in a driving school in Manila," I told Noel.

"Waste of money. You can learn here for free. Like me."

In the P.I., vehicles were expensive, and way beyond what the average Filipino could afford. Even middle-class folks could only afford second- or third-hand cars or "owners" which were modified stainless steel Jeeps. And anyway, public transportation was readily available: buses, "jeepneys," taxis, tricycles, pedicabs.

On Saipan, you just have to have a car. There were taxis but fares were ridiculously high. Later, enterprising Koreans and Chinese would offer cheap illegal taxi service. But when I first arrived on island, a private company that had tried to offer public transportation service had already shut down. There weren't a lot of customers in a place where most residents owned a vehicle. At that time, moreover, employers were required to provide transportation for their foreign workers, and Sam told me that I would be allowed to drive one of the company cars once I got my driver's license. In short, I had to learn how to drive, and Noel, bless his heart, volunteered to teach me.

But again, it wasn't like driving a bump car. That was fun because the goal was to hit other bump cars, and it was perfectly safe and even wickedly delightful. When driving a real car, the goal is not to hit anything—a daunting challenge when you're on a public road and there are lots of cars and pedestrians around you.

Noel was patient, however. He taught me the basics and explained local traffic rules, the right of way when shifting lanes, and the importance of obeying the STOP sign. He said in the P.I., there was only one rule: don't hit anything, and traffic lanes were "friendly suggestions" like traffic lights: green, go; yellow, go faster; and red, go if you can. On Saipan, Noel said, traffic lights were literal. If you try to beat a red light, a cop will give you a ticket. If you drive without a license, you get a ticket. If you drive too fast, you get a ticket. And if you drink and drive and you get caught, you'll end up in jail.

Noel had to explain all this to me because back in the P.I., erring drivers could just bribe a cop. On Saipan, Noel said, cops were known to report bribery attempts.

I learned how to drive in less than a month. I practiced every chance I got even in the evenings. The trickiest part, it turned out, was passing the driving test. The written test was ridiculously easy. Convincing the local cop that you could drive was hard. I failed the first time because he said my rear bumper was sagging. He failed me the second time because I ran a red light and parked the wrong way. He wanted to fail me the third time for driving, he said, like his great-grandma, but I told myself enough is enough; I have to take a stand. So I begged him. "Sir," I said, "my employer will be really mad at me if I fail again." I probably looked sufficiently pathetic because the officer said, "*Lanya*, go get your license. And don't hit anything out there when you drive."

A second-hand black 1991 Mazda Protegé. That was the company car I was allowed to use. It belonged to a former elected official who lost in the previous election and couldn't pay for his campaign ads our newspaper published. So our publisher, Sam, got his car.

"Don't drink and drive," Sam said to me.

"All right!" Noel said.

"Do you want Jesus to be your personal savior?" Joel asked of me.

23

THE political party of the newly elected governor gained seats in the House and the Senate, but not enough to form majorities. The governor was elected on a reform platform and had already lined up several pieces of controversial legislation, which included a reorganization of the executive branch and a tax hike, and he wanted them passed as soon as possible. But the opposition leaders who controlled the House and the Senate refused to play ball. Or, as Manny would put it, the price of their cooperation was just too high. So now the governor's allies in both chambers were planning a coup with the help of some of the opposition members themselves.

"But aren't the Senate president and House speaker cousins of the governor?" I asked.

"Who isn't," Manny replied.

"Why would opposition members support the governor's party?" I was so young.

"Because everyone likes carrots, and the governor has lots of them—and a big stick."

"Elected officials should act based on principles." I was so young and silly.

Manny laughed. "Good one. You still a commie? Anyway, they are acting on principle. And the principle is to get re-elected."

I would soon learn that the kind of politics and politicians that we all thought were the norm only existed in Frank Capra movies. In his world, there were cynical if not corrupt officials, to be sure, but there were also crusaders who could and would rise to the occasion and be carried on the shoulders of a virtuous people as they all head into the sunset.

But as a beat reporter who covered politics, I would eventually realize that politicians, including the people's advocates, are human beings, too. It turns out that they, too, act based on deeply personal preferences and they can hold personal grudges. They, too, can be needy, envious, slighted, flattered. They can confuse expediency with principle. They are calculating but are prone to miscalculation—like the rest of us. And for many of them, political labels are meaningless because, in the end, it's all about power. Because power can be used for the good of the many, power must be acquired by any means necessary as long as you can get away with it. And once you're in power, you use it to retain power.

"Serving the people." "For the betterment of the country." "For the sake of the nation."

"Who are the 'people,' the 'country,' the 'nation'?" Sam once asked me. "Did they all agree with what the politicians are doing in their name? People know next to nothing about a lot of things. That's why they elect officials who are supposed to know more. But once in office these politicians have little choice but to pander to the 'people'— or to the majority of voters whose minds will usually change in the next elections."

For the planned coup in the Legislature, Manny said the governor's point men were our friends, Representative Juan Acosta and Senator Leon Guzman.

"It will happen first in the Senate when they hold a session this week," Manny told me. "I'm guessing they'll make their move before adjournment. But you have to be there early just to be sure you won't miss anything."

In the House, the membership was based on the population of each of the three main islands. Saipan, the most populous, held 16 of the 18 seats with one each for Rota and Tinian. In the Senate, however, the three main islands were represented equally: three each. This was to ensure that Rota and Tinian would get more than just crumbs during the annual budget deliberations.

In the Senate, six members were with the opposition and three were with the governor's party. Two opposition members, however, were "ripe" for defection, Manny said. As the longest-serving political reporter on island, he was well-known in the local community and had many sources in the government. Manny was usually a step or two ahead of the other reporters.

"Once it's done I'll ask Guzman to help us with *Tun* Jack," Manny said. It had been almost a week since we last talked to the old man who was supposed to give us a call to arrange another meeting, and this time in sober daylight.

"He hasn't called?" I asked.

"I hope he's still alive. Anyway, Guzman's his nephew, but I can't bother him about *Tun* Jack right now. But once the deed's done, I will."

THE Senate session started late, at 3 p.m., because the Senate president and the floor leader had a behind-closed-door lengthy discussion about the session agenda. The floor leader wanted to include several items which the Senate president said could be discussed in another session. The Senate president was a veteran politician, and like other veteran politicians all over the world he could sense approaching danger. "Why are we having this goddamn conversation," he asked the floor leader, according to Guzman who would later tell me, off the record, what happened before the fateful session. The floor leader, it turned out, was among the plotters. The Senate vice president, too.

When the session finally began, the Senate president looked glum—if not disgusted—and he barely glanced at his floor leader who made one motion after another regarding the items on the agenda. Boring stuff. But the tension in the freezing Senate chamber was unmistakable. After the passage of the last of the bills listed on the agenda, the Senate president asked the floor leader to move for adjournment.

"Mr. President," the floor leader said, "I have a resolution to introduce." At which point, his staffer entered the chamber and began handing out copies of the resolution to all the members including the Senate president who didn't even read it. The resolution called for the election of a new Senate president.

"Motion to adjourn carried," the Senate president said.

"Mr. President," the floor leader said, "no one moved for adjournment."

"Session adjourned." The Senate president banged his gavel and went out of the chamber.

"*Lanya!*" Guzman said as he proceeded to speak in rapid, high-pitched Chamorro, so many words, none of which, I was sure, was flattering to the Senate president. All the other senators were standing up, but three of them soon walked out to join the Senate president in his office.

The five co-conspirators huddled with the Senate legal counsel. Guzman then told the reporters in the gallery, "We'll convene in the office of Senator Trinidad," referring to their newly elected, freshman member. (I later learned that no one else wanted to be the new Senate president and incur the wrath of the Senate president who was related to a huge family of voters. But Trinidad, who was new in politics, agreed to be the fall guy. He would never win an election again.)

So we followed the senators to Trinidad's office which was next door to the men's restroom.

The Senate vice president, as acting president, declared the resumption of the session, and the floor leader introduced his resolution which was adopted by all five members. The floor then nominated Trinidad for Senate president and he was elected unanimously. The first thing he did was to adjourn the session.

Me and the other reporters were about to interview him when a staffer of the ousted Senate president barged into Trinidad's office and said, "The Senate president is holding a press conference." So we reporters went with the staffer who ushered us into a conference room. The ousted leader, who was seated at the head of a long table, waited for the TV and radio reporters to set up their microphones while the print reporters took photos. Our photographer Malik was with me and was clicking away.

"I remain the Senate president," said the ousted Senate president, "and what they're doing now in Senator Trinidad's office is illegal. It is only fitting that they're doing it near the restroom because they're full of it."

Laughter.

"I will take them to court," he said and stood up. He wasn't taking any questions.

Before Malik and I left the legislative building, Senator Guzman approached me and said he had just talked with my editor Manny over the phone.

"You guys should have told me earlier," Guzman said. "I could have asked *Tun* Jack to be here during the session. But I don't know where he is now. I will call you or Manny once I find out."

"Thank you sir," I said.

"Is this about Amelia Earhart?"

I nodded.

"The old man knows something about it."

25

THE House coup should have been a walk in the park for the conspirators, but at the very last moment, they settled for the appearance of the status quo. What happened was that the House speaker, facing the inevitable, offered to step down during a session. Everyone knew what was going to happen, and so the gallery that day was packed with political supporters and kibitzers. The speaker decided that he would go out in a blaze of glory. He spoke in English first and then in Chamorro. He said titles meant nothing to him, and that all he wanted to do was to serve the people, and to protect their interests which was why he would not be the lackey of certain powerful politicians, an obvious dig at his cousin, the governor. Then the speaker related what his mother used to tell him about public service. His voice cracked and he began to tear up.

That was it. The speaker's other cousin who was supposed to be the new presiding officer took the floor, and spoke in Chamorro, affirming his respect and love for the man he was about to expel from the speakership. Then he sobbed and cried.

Next was the leader of the coup plotters, the vice speaker who was also a cousin of the speaker. He, too, spoke in Chamorro, pledging his undying support for family values, the local culture and the local people. He said he, too, loved his cousin, the speaker. Then he cried.

"*Lanya* these guys," Senator Guzman would later tell me. "In the Senate, we shoot to kill. In the House, crybabies." He laughed.

It turned out that there was no need to oust the speaker. The coup plotters simply turned him into a figurehead while they set a legislative agenda that reflected the governor's.

There was more drama when lawmakers began deliberating on his reorganization and tax-hike proposals. The ousted Senate president, whose lawsuit against his ouster was dismissed by the court, and the defanged House speaker spoke against the measures, called the governor dictatorial, if not Satanic, and warned that he would usher in a new Dark Age. Despite the public outcry, or what appeared to be public outcry, the proposals easily passed both houses. Those were the days when, to express your outrage, you must call your legislator or write a letter to the editor. Now we have Twitter and Facebook and online comments that can be posted on newspaper articles. Now everyone is a pundit. Now you can be heard immediately, your resentments re-tweeted and re-posted and capable of reaching millions of people all over the world like a never-ending echo. Now public outcry is like a water faucet—no; a dam!— that you can turn on or off at will. Public outcry as an inundation. A flood of biblical proportions but without an ark.

But back then, a public outcry was difficult to sustain especially since the local economy continued to improve as new businesses opened one after the other, and more tourists from Japan and South Korea arrived each day, and more orders for "Made in USA" apparel manufactured on Saipan were placed by The Gap, Ralph Lauren and Tommy Hilfiger among other famous brand names. The local government, like other governments all over the world that was awash with cash, went on a spending and hiring spree. The governor threw money at everyone, even at his critics…who ceased to be critical.

26

EVERY week-day, we had to be at the office before 9 in the morning, and from there I would head to the governor's office and the nearby legislative building. The area was called Capitol Hill, named after, we all assumed, the landmark building in the American capital. But according to a retired local government official, we were wrong. The name was *Capital* Hill. During the Trust Territory era, he said, Saipan was the capital of the TT government, and most of its offices were on that hill. Hence, Capital Hill. But eventually, on this island of goodbyes, many assumed that "Capital" was a typo and "Capitol" was the "correct" word. So even today, most people refer to it as Capitol Hill even though there is no Capitol on that hill.

It was difficult to keep track of things on an island where the chroniclers of "facts" or "news" came and went, and their replacements naturally would start back in the proverbial Year Zero, again and again. For newly arrived reporters, everything was new. But it was not so, and they just didn't know it. The past was a memory of a rumor—or a rumor of a memory. And those who knew could only offer disjointed recollections of older people's recollections.

If news reporting was supposed to set the tone for the public discussion of the burning issues of the day, then I don't think island reporters, many of whom were basically parachute journalists, did a good job. Local or stateside reporters, sooner or later, would be hired by the government as public information officers. And most if not all stateside reporters would eventually move back to the states. As for Filipino reporters, they, too, would one day leave and return to the P.I. or, if they could, head to greener pastures like Guam or the states where they would usually end up in a different career like caregiving.

Manny was different. "Know the history of this place," he would tell me. "You must be aware of what happened before. And always follow the money. How they get funding. How they spend it. More important: don't gossip about a local person to another local person because chances are they're related. You want to be a 'serious' writer, right?" He brought me to the island's public library one day, and I thought I would cry out loud, seeing all those beautiful hardbound books and learning that I could borrow any of them. I felt like a kid with a lot of money in a toy store. I couldn't decide, but I finally chose Thomas Wolfe's *Look Homeward Angel* and Thomas Pynchon's *Gravity's Rainbow*.

Manny said: "Serious writers take their craft seriously. Same thing with covering a beat. Treat it with respect. Never assume you already know it all. Always, *always*, double check. Of course that's easier said than done. But we have to do it." He added, "I probably would have been a good seaman."

As for the elusive *Tun* Jack, Senator Guzman finally brought him to his office where we met the old man again. Even before Manny could ask him about Amelia Earhart, *Tun* Jack said he wanted us to help his "friend," a Filipina "exotic dancer," as they were called on Saipan, at Hot Stuff, a popular girly bar.

Senator Guzman, who was from another island, said he couldn't help his friend because it was a Saipan issue— and the building owner was a cousin. But the bar itself was owned by a Filipino couple, U.S. citizens from Guam.

Tun Jack wanted us to write about the "abused" dancers. He said their employers were holding onto the dancers' passports. The girls couldn't leave their barracks, which was on the second floor of a building, without getting permission from the owners. They were also told that if they got pregnant they would be sent home right away.

"Interview my friend *lai*, put it in the news, and then we talk again about Amelia Earhart," *Tun* Jack said.

"But you do know something about her, right," Manny asked, "Amelia Earhart."

"*Lanya*, I know a lot about what happened to her."

27

B Y the time I had left the P.I., horror stories about abused Filipino workers abroad, especially in the Middle East, were staple news stories and a plot feature of many tear-jerkers on TV and the big screen.

Construction workers and maids raped in Saudi Arabia. Maids beaten up by their employers in Hong Kong or Singapore. Bar girls in Japan who ended up working for the Yakuza. Yet more and more Filipinos, if given the chance, chose to work abroad. It really didn't matter where. Nigeria. Lebanon. Cyprus. The Federated States of Micronesia. Palau. Iraq. Libya.

We all knew that when we worked abroad, we could get into trouble. But then again, working overseas meant way higher salaries, thanks to the exchange rate. Moreover, for every abused overseas Filipino worker, nine prospered: they managed to send their kids to good colleges, even bought a new home or rebuilt an old one, and started their own businesses.

Many of us liked the odds. We were willing to take our chances. Especially on Saipan where most of the reported abuses—which, to begin with, weren't sensational enough for the Philippine media—were basically breach-of-contract disputes: delayed release of pay checks; failure to pay overtime; illegal deductions; poor working conditions. There were also allegations of forced prostitution among bar workers. And, among Chinese garment workers, forced abortions. "Under the American flag!" human rights advocates thundered. "Shame on U.S. soil!"

U.S. national publications had a field day. *The New York Times*, *The Washington Post*, *Reader's Digest*, *Time* magazine, the major TV networks and at least two U.S. novels: one of which depicted Saipan as the "island of slaves," while the other sensationalized the already sensational labor-abuse stories on the neighboring island of Rota.

In the Northern Marianas, the foreign employees most vulnerable to abuse were maids and bar girls, many of whom were, more or less, treated like indentured servants. The only way we could talk with *Tun* Jack's "friend" was to see her at the club where she worked, and buy her drinks. Manny said this time, I had to be on my own because the club owners might recognize him. He gave me enough money to buy *Tun* Jack's friend two drinks. I met her on Monday evening, around 9 a.m. There weren't a lot of people there yet. Her stage name was Maja—Spanish "j" which is pronounced like an "h." She was about 5 feet and 3 inches tall and probably weighed less than 100 pounds. Small eyes, small nose, ready smile and a Visayan accent. Stateside Americans would have found her adorable. *Tun* Jack worshipped her.

I asked her many questions about her concerns, but she seemed more interested in the old man's finances. Was he rich? Had I ever been in his house? How many cars did he have? What about his kids? How many? Did they still live with him?

Maja said she was thinking about running away from her employers, the husband and wife, and "hooking up"—her words—with *Tun* Jack. She said she had to make sure that she would not be jumping from the frying fan into the fire. She was afraid that her employers would deport her as they had threatened to do. I told her only the government could deport her. She said her employers had many friends in high places, specifically in the labor department and the immigration division whose officials were usually given free drinks whenever they were in the club. She was hoping that *Tun* Jack had friends in *higher* places.

I told her the old man was related to at least one influential lawmaker, but I wasn't too sure if he was "loaded." At this point, she appeared to be sunk in thought.

"I have two brothers still in elementary and middle school," she said as if talking about the weather. "My father left us when we were still kids. I didn't even finish high school. My mother's a maid and works for our town mayor. But she's getting too old for that job. I really thought that if I work here, things would finally get better for us. But my employers are horrible people. I can't do anything without their permission. We can't go out after work. We can't go out even on our days off unless…"

"Unless what?"

"Someone buys us a $100 champagne in the VIP room," and she pointed to one of the three doors near the stage.

I had to ask. "Do they *do* it there?"

She laughed. "Those doors don't have locks. Those are swinging doors. But maybe some find that more exciting." She laughed again.

"Maybe your employers will ease up a bit if I write a news story about how they run this place."

"Sure."

"You don't think it's a good idea."

"What I think is that they'll get mad, fire all of us, bring us to the airport and send us home."

"And if you run away with *Tun* Jack?"

"He'll help me file a labor complaint. Maybe I can get another job." She sighed. "You can earn good money here, you know, with the tips. But I really can't stand my employers anymore."

I said nothing.

"How old is the old man?" she asked.

"I don't know. In his 60s?"

"He's very kind, you know. Like a grandpa."

"How old are you?"

"Don't tell anyone."

"Okay."

"I'm 18. My permit says 21."

"When did you arrive here?"

"About a year ago."

"You were 17?"

"Sixteen turning 17 but I looked older."

"Oh crap."

"Come on. Seventeen is already too old if you're a dancer in the P.I."

She was exaggerating, but it's partly true: I'd known bar girls and dancers who were barely in their teens. Which was, of course, against the law even in the Philippines.

"What was your age when you lost your virginity" she asked.

"I'm still a virgin."

She laughed. She laughed like she was already an old woman. Or was it I who was growing older as I sat there with her, sipping my one and only bottle of Miller Light, which cost $5, while she twirled the small umbrella of her $14 "lady's drink"? (Her club didn't have a $7 "single" drink.)

"What's that anyway?' I asked.

"Iced tea."

"Comes from a can?"

"It's Lipton tea with sugar."

"Hah."

"That's the only other thing I like about my job."

"What do you mean?"

"In the P.I. the lady's drink is beer."

"Yeah."

"I'd get drunk after just two bottles. And whenever I had more I'd just end up puking my guts out."

I chuckled.

"And beer makes you fat."

"You're not going to be fat."

She smiled. "You're sweet."

"Just saying."

"And cute, too."

I chuckled again.

"How long have you been here?" she asked.

"Almost a year."

"You got a wife?"

"Single."

"Even in the P.I.?"

I laughed. "I do have a girlfriend."
"But she's over there."
"Yes"
"So far away." Smiling with her eyes now.
I believe I smiled back.

28

MY typical work-day would end at 7 p.m. I was still not hungry because I would usually order food from our office kitchen throughout the afternoon. I couldn't get enough of our lunch lady's *siomai*, the Chinese dumpling that Filipinos love. She would sprinkle it with crushed, deep fried garlic and served it with the glorious local sauce, *finadene*—Kikkoman soy sauce, lemon juice or vinegar, chopped green and white onions and chili pepper. Then there was *soba*: instant noodle soup topped with slices of Spam and cabbage, pickled red ginger and raw egg which, after a while, wasn't that raw anymore.

Late in the evening, if I was suddenly hungry, I would drive down to the nearest store and buy Pringles and grapes for less than five dollars. American candy bars and other snack items, including Ben & Jerry's ice cream, were also available at most of the mom and pop stores. These items could be bought in the P.I., but were sold in fancy malls and were too expensive for common folks.

Food was the least of concerns for those on island. There was usually food during media events, and weekend gatherings were always about food. It seemed that we could run out of a lot of things but not food.

The big problem was loneliness. It would hit you—bitch-slap you—when you were in your room during yet another seemingly never-ending evening. I would try to read, but after a while, I couldn't focus on the words anymore, and I would miss Sweet, her physical presence, and my friends, and even my mother and my sister and my brother, and the noise and pollution of Manila. I would end up staring at the ceiling or the wall, in the dark, my mind lost in labyrinthine thoughts, and then it would be 6 a.m. when I was about to give in to sleep, but instead I had to go shower and get ready for work.

Of course I could drink myself into a stupor every night, but even I knew it wasn't a good idea—the hangover and damaged liver—the F. Scott Fitzgerald of it all but with neither his talent nor literary output.

I couldn't call Sweet all the time. It cost too much. There were no phone cards yet. Once, we talked for over an hour, and my phone bill was around $175. So I wrote her long, laser-printed letters I composed on my office Mac computer. Her letters were hand-written, and she wrote in script which was not elegant, but legible. She used scented writing paper in pastel colors. It took two weeks or more before we got our letters. In those days, what were considered technological wonders were fax machines and alpha-numeric pagers.

Eventually, I heeded my co-workers' advice and bought a TV, a VCR and a CD/cassette player and radio for less than $2,000. Lay away! I just had to make a $100 downpayment and leave my passport with the appliance store owner, a Filipino-American from Guam. Each payday, I handed him $100 and once I paid what I owed he would return my passport.

I also signed up for cable TV service which included the P.I.'s ABS-CBN channel, but the programs, like those from the American networks aired in Hawaii, were shown a week late. Still, it was better than staring at the wall. Anyway, if I wanted the latest news about the old country, I could go to this Filipino store that sold Philippine newspapers and magazines that would arrive on island after 5 p.m., brought in on the last flight from Manila. The *Philippine Daily Inquirer* was a buck each, the tabloids were 50 cents each and the magazine I loved, mainly because of its literary section, *Philippines Free Press,* was a dollar-fifty.

We all looked forward to Fridays. We published Monday to Friday only, which meant we worked Sunday to Thursday. I still had to cover my beats on Fridays, but the pace was more relaxed, the day held so much promise…of what exactly?

Of fun, I guess. Of forgetting one's loneliness—of the thought at the back of your mind that you were with strangers on foreign land, thousands of miles away from home. No relatives or familiar friends in sight. No one knew you.

Which gave me the idea, of all things, to grow my hair long. Eddie Vedder long. Those were the days when I listened, as much as I could, to the music of Pearl Jam, Nirvana, Alice in Chains, Soundgarden, Candle Box. I watched grunge-era *Singles* on video countless times.

Self-pity wasn't my thing. I preferred to sulk—but only when I was alone. Besides, there was so much to see on this small island: the beaches, the historic and other tourist sites, and there were so many people to meet, so many cultures to encounter. At times I forgot that I was there to work and that I was not a tourist.

29

FOR the Filipinos on the island, the Sunday Mass and the gatherings on the beach were their social life. Noel told me he used to attend morning Mass every week, but he got tired of the priest's sermons. Most of the priests were Filipinos, and lately, I was told, they had been scolding adulterers from their pulpit.

"What would be surprising is if they preached fornication," Manny told Noel at the office, at the end of another long news day. "But they're priests so what do you expect."

"They're hypocrites," Noel said.

"Well," Manny replied.

Noel already had a girlfriend who, Manny and I believed, was about to be pregnant. Noel was practically shacking up with her at her barracks. She was a waitress.

"Hypocrites!" Noel said again. "And some of them think we don't know they're in the closet!"

"That's why the Bible alone should be our guide," Joel said.

"Amen," Manny said like he was uttering a curse.

And then there were the pot-luck gatherings at the beach on weekends. Ice-cold beer and soda. Barbecued ribs or chicken, rice and, of course, *pancit*, the Filipino noodle dish invented in the P.I. by Chinese immigrants during the Spanish era.

Incidentally, rice on Saipan was far superior to what we had in the P.I. First of all, it was from California and you could buy it in yellow bags of various sizes and weight. You didn't need to "wash" it. This rice no longer had husks or ash, and those tiny black pebbles that came from God knows where. Moreover, California rice and Filipino *ulam* or dishes were a heavenly match. California rice, or Calrose, had the texture, the softness and the stickiness that either disclosed or heightened the full flavors of pork *adobo*, for example. Such rice, as with many other good things in life, was also available in the Philippines, but it was expensive. (Not surprisingly, those who were very rich would never dream of leaving the P.I. unless it was to go on vacation, flee scandal or repression.)

In my early days on Saipan, everyone wanted to talk to me during the get-togethers on the beach. They would ask me for the "latest" news, particularly about showbiz scandals and gossip of which, I had to admit, I knew a lot. I received a lot of invitations to join the various Filipino groups on island. There were groups based on one's region back home. There were groups based on your profession. Then there were the Bible study groups and the church choirs or the sports club: tennis, badminton, billiards, darts, cycling and even chess.

Later, as your social circle expanded, your local friends might ask you to join their bowling team or the golf club. The statesiders had their music society, their writers group, the friends of the library and the Hash House Harriers—a "drinking club with a running problem." Hashing, I was told, was "invented" in the late 1930s by a bunch of drunken Brits in then-British Malaya. The supposed goal was to get rid of one's hangover by running all over the forest. It was so effective that they decided to celebrate by drinking themselves into a coma. On Saipan, you and a bunch of other people (mostly statesiders and their Asian or local friends) had to follow a trail through the boonies, the goal being to reach a beach site where there would be a huge bonfire and everyone would try to pass out drinking beer while singing redneck music. Or so I was told.

For Filipinos back home, drinking was a social event. Everyone had to drink the same amount of whatever it was they were drinking: beer or liquor. They drank from the same glass, and someone was in charge of filling the glass with the agreed-upon amount of alcohol, and everyone would get their turn, and round and round the glass went. Drinking, in other words, was a social chore. In contrast, the statesiders I met on Saipan considered drinking as something that relaxed you. And it was up to you what you drank and how much. I knew a stateside lawyer who, before the start of dinner, would begin with what he called an *aperitif*: a shot of single malt whisky. (At that point in my life all alcoholic drinks that were not beer tasted like melted aluminum to me.) He would eat his meal with either red or white wine, depending on what the food was. After dessert, he would have brandy. He said he was appalled to see people—meaning Filipinos—putting ice in beer, wine, champagne or brandy. That's not even barbaric, he said; it's a sacrilege. His name was Rob Fisher. He taught me how to drink.

We first met at a hotel poolside gathering hosted by the governor's office for visiting Japanese businessmen. He saw me looking at the glass of red wine a waiter offered me. I took a sip. I grimaced. I was a beer drinker. An *iced* beer drinker.

"When you've had enough of that fancy stuff, you may want to try a real man's drink." Rob said, raising his glass of Chivas Regal—"neat"; no ice.

We had seen each other before. He was legal counsel to one of the executive departments. He looked like he was in his early 30s. Many Caucasian Americans tend to look older than their actual age. U.S lawyers on Saipan, like cable TV reporters and anchors, are often in their early 20s when they first arrive. They surely don't come here for the pay which is much less than what they could get in the states. But many believe that working on a faraway tropical island is an interesting proposition. Low tax rates. Free housing if you work for the government. And your lack of experience is not counted against you. For TV reporters, they could be fresh out of the college, but on Saipan they are given major beat assignments *and* become anchors right away. And on weekends: stunning beaches and diving sites, all-year-round tropical weather, a variety of cultures, and an overall sense that time is taking its time on an island where everything seems to be moving, if at all, leisurely.

30

ROB Fisher said he was from Oak Park, west of Chicago, Illinois. "Where Ernest Hemingway was born," he told me. He said he got his political science and law degrees from the University of Illinois where he was a member of the Young Republicans.

"You were an activist in college?" he once asked me during yet another government function at another hotel poolside.

"Oh yeah." I said.

"Of what sort?

"There's only one type of activist back home: commies."

"Really."

"But there's also social democrats or 'democratic socialists.' " Air quotes.

"And what do you commies call them?" Rob was grinning.

"Clerico-fascist, counter-revolutionary swine."

We laughed.

Rob's girlfriend was the Filipina maid/baby-sitter of an engineer from the states who worked for another executive branch department. The engineer and his wife, also from the states, had two young kids. They were Rob's neighbors on Capital Hill.

Rob loved his girlfriend, Mila, which he thought was spelled the way she pronounced it, "Meehla." Whenever we saw each other, he would ask me about certain things said or done by Mila that puzzled him.

"She cooked me tamarind-broth stew with leafy vegetables and shrimp."

"Yummy."

"The shrimp's unshelled and she didn't remove the head!"

I laughed.

"Did she do that on purpose? Is she mad at me?"

"That's the way it's cooked back home."

"Really."

What, he asked, was the "crap" that she usually served him when he wanted coffee?

"That would be instant coffee," I said.

"Newly boiled water!"

"That's how we drink it."

"I scalded my mouth!"

"And now you know better."

Rob also asked me what the "deal" was with using spoon and fork. "Why must I always ask her for a knife? And I think she believes summer is March and April."

"Well, it is back home."

"Your summer is in spring?"

"We don't have summer. We're in the tropics remember? We only have dry and wet seasons. But we call our dry season 'summer' because who the hell wants to go on a 'dry season' vacation?"

He chuckled.

Rob would sometimes call me at the office if he had questions about whatever new puzzling "Filipino thing" Mila had sprung on him.

"She snickers every time I say 'pennies.' "

I laughed.

"What?"

"Back home, some people pronounce 'penis' 'pennies.' "

"Why the hell do they do that?"

So I had to explain how the Philippine language "worked": you pronounce the vowels one way only. "E" is always "e" as in "egg." "A" is always "a" in "apple." Etc. And "f" is "p"; "v" is "b"; "z" is "s."

"I should be charging for all this info," I said, smiling.

"You should teach a course at the local college. 'How to be Married to a Filipina 101.' "

"How did you guys meet anyway?" I asked.

"Hah. Yeah. That was memorable. Went up to Ted's house." Ted was his engineer friend. "Knocked on the door, and it was Mila who opened it. Love at first sight swear to God." Mila was about 5'1", brown-skinned, thin, long black hair, big brown eager eyes.

"I asked her if Ted was around. And she said (her words): 'He just come back but then he pass away'!"

"Ah." I was smiling.

"So I said, 'Oh my God! When? How did it happen? Where are Wendy and the kids?' And she was looking at me smiling, probably thought I was nuts."

"When did you finally understand what she just told you?" I was already laughing.

"When she told me Ted would be back in a few minutes, with Wendy and the kids."

It was through Mila that Rob learned about an "explosive" news story that he wanted me to "uncover."

"I shouldn't even be seen talking to you in public, do you know that?" Rob told me over the phone.

"Well that doesn't happen a lot anyway."

"Yeah, and when it does it's usually a public event anyway."

"So?"

"It's big."

"All ears."

"Mila's friends with the governor's two maids."

"Okay."

"They're not getting paid."

"No way!"

"Not even a cent for three months now."

"That's not possible."

"Exactly. The governor's office pays their salaries through a manpower agency."

Local law restricts government hiring of nonresidents. Hence, the maids were hired through an agency owned by a U.S. citizen.

"Guess who?" Rob asked.

"Spill."

"The TV cameraman, Jerry."

"Crap."

"Yeah, crap."

Jerry was a statesider who had been a cook, a bartender, helicopter mechanic and now a news cameraman at one of the two cable TV stations. He was in his late 30s and married to a Filipina, a former hotel waitress. They had no kids, but they had a manpower business. Mila told Rob that Mrs. Jerry was addicted to video poker and was apparently gambling away the maids' paychecks.

"Does the governor know?" I asked.

"Probably. The first lady learned about it because the maids asked her if they could each borrow $20 or something. Of course the first lady asked them why. So she learned that there's this scandalous situation happening under the very nose of her husband who has been assuring the feds that his administration will not tolerate labor abuses." Rob laughed.

"Jerry's a nice guy," I said.

"I bet his wife's a nice lady, too," Rob said.

"Scoop!" I said.

"Pulitzer!" Rob said.

"But what if the governor denies it?"

"Yeah. About that. They could rip up the contract with Jerry's wife, get another manpower agency to hire the maids, who should have gotten their back wages already."

"But it's still a story!"

"If the governor confirms."

"He's not stupid."

"That he's not. Interview the maids! But I don't think they'll talk to you."

"Yeah. I bet they love their gig."

"And if they're paid already and assured of regular, timely payments…"

"But what a story!"

"Not as big," Rob said, "as Amelia Earhart's though."

31

I N the P.I., I'd heard stories of Filipino workers in Saudi Arabia who, after work, with nothing much to do at their barracks, would gamble to while their time away. Maybe the fact that gambling was illegal there made it more exciting. So some gambled all the time, and the very few lucky ones who won enough tore up their job contracts and booked the next flight back to Manila. Eventually, they would be looking for new jobs abroad, of course.

A Philippine TV magazine program once sent a crew to Saipan to do a feature on the lives of the Filipinos there. "Island of Sin" was the title of the Saipan episode, and it depicted Filipinos gambling at the cockpit or the poker arcades, hitting the strip joints, having second families, drinking beer at the beach—as if life on the island should be more virtuous; as if there should be no vices there.

It was the same thing with newly arrived statesiders who were usually "shocked" to read about child abuse and other domestic cases, burglaries and government corruption happening on Saipan. As if illegal behavior and acts should—*must*—never happen on the island, especially while they were there.

Saipan was a peaceful community. Police officers were quick to respond to any calls for help. The high and mighty could be, and were, charged with felonies. Murders, and they could happen on a small island, were always considered shocking and intolerable—but they were rare.

As for gambling, it bored me. But I'm quite sure it's like TV soap operas. You sneer at them, their ridiculous plots, the ham actors and their "avid watchers," then you watch one or two episodes, then three and four, and before you know it you're hooked yourself.

It was also too expensive to go to a strip joint every week.

Happily, I liked to read. I signed up for book club memberships through the mail and I also became a regular library patron. I also had cable TV and a VCR. But after a while, loneliness—not boredom—would set in. So on Fridays and Saturdays, I did look forward to hanging out with Noel and Manny whenever our boss, Sam, would invite us to his house for a drink. Sam was partial to white wine which he served chilled and with various kinds of cheese he liked to order from the states. Sam was more of a listener than a talker. I talked a lot inebriated or not. Noel and Manny, not so much—until the second or third glass of white wine. And then Sam, like a symphony conductor, would urge us to contribute to the conversation lest it became a lecture. I learned from Noel that Sam used to invite Joel to these drinking sessions, but Joel seemed unable to stop himself from attempting to convert his employer and co-workers and bring them back to Jesus. Malik our photographer was Muslim, but he didn't mind getting drunk now and then. Sadly, a month or so after I arrived on Saipan, he joined some of his friends, Bangladeshis and Filipinos, in boarding a plane to Japan where they became illegal aliens who, I was told, earned really good money as construction workers.

"What do you think you'd be if you weren't a journalist," Sam once asked us, sipping his white wine, nibbling cheese he said was called Gruyere.

"A chess player," Manny said, who, it turned out, was a frustrated woodpusher.

"Basketball player," Noel said.

"A drummer in a rock band," I said.

"I would probably be a gardener," our employer said. He added, "Amelia Earhart wrote newspaper articles. She had a gap-toothed smile, I read somewhere…. Manny, where are we with that story?"

"Maybe Benjie should tell you," my editor said, looking at me, grinning. I could tell that he was amused at how my face could so suddenly become red.

"Benjie?" my boss asked.

"Uh," I said.

Noel laughed. He knew. I told Manny about it, but I didn't tell Noel. But of course he knew. Perhaps everyone at the barracks knew.

"I don't think *Tun* Jack would want to talk to us now," Manny said, still smiling.

"Why the hell not?" our boss said, looking at me.

"Uh," I said.

"Our lover boy is loving the old man's love," Noel said, laughing at his own unfunny joke.

"What?" Sam looked irritated.

"Uh," I said.

"He's dating *Tun* Jack's girlfriend from the bar," Manny said.

Noel laughed like a loon.

"What?"

"And by dating, I mean he's boinking her every now and then."

"Uh."

"Goddamnit Benjie."

"Uh."

32

NOEL was no longer in a laughing mood after his wife learned about his girlfriend on island—and the fact that the other woman had just given birth to their baby boy. "Someone ratted on me," he said in the newsroom, early in the evening. Manny was reading some of the "camera-ready" pages for tomorrow's edition before they were brought down to the production department. I was at my desk, reading, or trying to read, if not decipher, *Finnegans Wake*, a copy of which I borrowed from the library. This was before the advent of Amazon.com, and I wasn't aware that there were books that could guide me through Joyce's riddle wrapped in a mystery inside an enigma hurled into a well within a labyrinth in the middle of godknowswhere.

As the lion in our teargarten remembers the nenuphars of his Nile (shall Ariuz forget Arioun or Boghas the baregams of the Marmarazalles from Marmeniere?) it may be, tots wearsense full a naggin in twentyg have sigilposted what in our brievingbust, the besieged bedreamt him stil and solely of those lililiths undeveiled which hat undone him, gone for age, and knew not the watchful treachers at his wake, and theirs to stay. Fooi, fooi, chamermissies! Zeepyzoepy, larcenlads! Zijnzijn Zijnzijn! It may be, we moest ons hasten selves te declareer it, that he reglimmed? presaw? the fields of heat and yields of wheat where corngold Ysit? shamed and shone.

My thoughts exactly.

"I don't know why some people can't mind their own business." Noel was seated at his desk, looking at the blank screen of his Mac. He had heard an earful from his wife earlier that day. She called the office—collect which Noel had to accept. Every now and then he would say "No, no, no" while at the other end of the line his sobbing wife repeated—re-read—the contents of the letter she had received that day, mailed by someone from Saipan.

"I'm the last guy you should be talking to right now," Manny told Noel.

Of course Manny's wife back home already knew about his family on island. So now he was trying to divorce her.

"They have no right," Noel said, referring to whoever was the blabbermouth.

"He or she knows your mailing address in the P.I.," I offered.

"That's right," Noel said. "It could only be someone in the publisher's office, or someone who knows someone there."

"Didn't you have a shouting match with Linda?" I asked. She was the receptionist on the ground floor, a Filipina married to a local man. She liked to boss around the company's Filipino workers.

"She started it," Noel said.

"But you did call her an ugly bitch," Manny said.

"Actually," I said, "he said, 'you should put a paperbag over your head because you're a *paking* ugly bitch.' "

"She is!"

"What did you tell your wife?" I asked.

"I denied everything."

"That'll work," Manny said, his two thumbs pointing at himself.

"*Shet*," Noel said.

Why, Rob once asked me, do you guys pronounce it "*shet*"?

"Face it," Manny said. "It's over."

"My parents. Her parents. Our kid," Noel said.

"Should I say it, or should you," Manny told me.

"You've made your bed, now lie in it?" I said.

"Thanks guys," Noel said. "Really helpful."

"You never thought you'd get away with it, right," Manny said. "Not in this day and age."

"Not with these goddamn, low-class, fat-mouthed, mother—"

"Now, now; leave moms out of it," Manny said. It seemed that he was enjoying Noel's domestic quagmire.

"And you," Manny told me. "You better not pick a fight with Linda."

I chuckled. And then I blushed like a 13-year-old whose shorts were pulled down in front of his crush.

"I'm headed to the barracks," Noel said, not waiting for a reply, as he stood up and headed to the exit.

"Don't do anything stupid," Manny shouted. Pause. "I should have said, 'Don't commit another stupidity.'

Speaking of which, how the hell can we get any info from *Tun* Jack now?"

"I'll fix that," I said, not knowing how.

33

UN Jack's girl, Maja, the one I had been exceedingly friendly with in a moment of weakness—OK, so many moments of them; lots and lots of them—she "fixed" my problem. Men in love are always willing to believe whatever the beloved one tells them, and Maja—Weng, the "e" pronounced like the "e" in egg, and short for Rowena, her real name, the "e" again as in egg—turned out to be a spellbinding teller of tales. Scheherazade couldn't hold a candle to Weng.

She told *Tun* Jack that I had been interviewing her a lot (right, in the evening, the two of us in a room), because she wanted me to get the "facts" "right." But most of time, we ended up talking about him a lot. She considered me an older brother after all, and come on, let's get real here. He has a girlfriend (probably his wife for all we know), and in Manila, he still lives with his mom. What I need is a real man like you, who can give my life stability, who can guide me, who will love me for the rest of our lives....

And *Tun* Jack believed her because he wanted to. And maybe Weng believed what she was telling him at that very moment.

"How old is he exactly?" I once asked her. We were in bed in a motel that charged $20 for half a day. It was near, but not too near, her barracks which was behind their club. It was a week day, lunch-time. It was laundry day for her and the other girls who were at a Laundromat. I had to take her back there soon.

She never asked me for anything, but I would always bring her something whenever we saw each other. Food from McDonald's or Kentucky Fried Chicken. A shirt. A pair of shorts. Soap. And she would say, "How sweet my boyfriend," and laugh while I blushed.

"He's in his 60's, right?" I said, referring to her other boyfriend.

"I don't know. Maybe 62 or 63," Weng said, staring at the white ceiling. I was looking at my faded jeans, folded on the back of the chair at the table to my right, near the door to the restroom.

"Can he still do it?" I asked despite myself.

"You really want to know?"

Weng had been a bar girl since she was 13. At 18 she was a battle-scarred veteran of life already. She knew what men liked, and how to make them like what she liked.

She was familiar with our delusions, and we knew nothing about hers—or thought we did. In the P.I., she had a boyfriend, but just a few months after flying to Saipan, she learned that he was already with another woman.

"*Tun* Jack," I said.

"What."

"He can still do it?"

"He's into snuggling. And touching. And kissing."

"Eww."

She laughed. "He smells good, you know. Calvin Klein. And he's clean and he doesn't chew betel nut. Or he no longer does."

"Are you going to shack up with him?"

"I'm thinking about it." Pause. "Maybe I've got no choice."

"You must marry him."

"Of course."

"Green card and all."

"Sure."

"I'm going to write the news story about your labor complaint, if you're filing one."

"Oh I will. The other girls, one of them has an American boyfriend. He tells us we should sue our employers so we can get money—money that they owe us anyway."

"When will you file the complaint?"

"I'll tell you when."

"When can I talk to *Tun* Jack?"

"He's not mad at you."

"That's good."

"He just doesn't want to see you ever again." And she laughed.

I didn't say anything.

"Don't sulk," she said. "Just kidding. He'll talk to you. I'll make him talk to you." Now smiling which was the only thing she was wearing, and oh how she wore it.

I'M not a whore," Weng told me the first time we "went out." It was a sunny Friday morning. She and the other girls, all 10 of them, had to do their laundry. The bar owner, the husband, who drove a van, dropped them at the nearest Laundromat and would pick them up two hours later. There was more than enough time to "sneak out." The girls had an arrangement. Some of them would go somewhere else while the rest looked after their laundry. Next laundry day, it would be the turn of the other girls to "play truant" while the others took care of their laundry. What if the boss arrived while the other girls were still "out"? Everyone would say they were in one of the stores a few blocks away and would be back soon.

I was just about to leave for Capital Hill to cover my beats when she phoned. She told me where they were going—she was still at their barracks—and that I should pick her up so we could have lunch and then we could talk. Just you and me, she said. Oh, I said. I proceeded to the Laundromat, and there she was outside, seated on a wooden bench with some of the other girls, all pale, without make-up, their hair, dyed brown, tied in a pony-tail, looking their age which was from late teens to very early 20s.

Weng smiled—she seemed genuinely happy to see me—as the company car I was driving pulled into the parking lot. She was wearing a white Hello Kitty shirt, hotpants and pink metallic, rubber soled flip-flops with a slim thong strap. Like a child, she ran toward the sedan, opened the passenger door, plopped herself on the seat, put on the seat belt, and looked at me. She was beaming. "I thought you wouldn't show up," she said.

"For you, I'll do anything," I said, and was surprised that at that exact moment I was telling the truth.

"Yey!" she said.

After we bought snacks from a grocery store, I brought her to my room at the barracks, an eight-minute drive from the Laundromat. No one was at the barracks at the time. She liked my room. "It's like a beach cottage in the P.I.," she said. "And it so breezy here. And so many plants out there." From somewhere, a cow mooed. "It's like I'm in the province!" She added, "This is the first time I've gone out with a man." I really didn't care if that was true or not. "It's hard to be alone," she said. I couldn't argue with that. "And I like you. You're nice. And clean." "I thought I was cute, too," I said. She giggled.

She had been on island for over a year now, and had just reluctantly agreed to renew her contract for another year. That was before she met *Tun* Jack. She said she didn't have a lot of admirers among their regular customers. "All they want is a quickie, and they're gross and disrespectful." But there was this nice black American who would always "table" her every time he was on island, which wasn't frequently—he was with the Navy. She last saw him months ago.

"What if he shows up?" I asked.

"Ooooo, jealous."

"*Tun* Jack."

"The old man wants to marry me."

"First come, first served."

"Something like that. Unless."

"Unless what."

"You propose to me." And we laughed, and I wondered, why the hell not?

35

eng's employers got wind of the girls' plan to "run away" and file labor complaints. One of the girls squealed. She had a fight with another girl over a customer. Most of the other girls didn't take her side. So she ratted on them.

Weng said that after their employers threatened to haul them to the airport, there and then, she made a frantic phone call to *Tun* Jack who rushed to their barracks, Don Quixote on a dark-blue Nissan Pathfinder. He threatened the employers with a lawsuit while dropping the names of his relatives who were government officials, adding that he also had friends in the media. The employers, husband and wife, looked at each other. Then the mrs. told the old man that they didn't want any trouble. *Tun* Jack looked at Weng, who looked at him. She wanted to look dead-serious, she would later tell me. *Tun* Jack said he would like to confer with the girls. He was still standing outside the barracks, a one-story house with several rooms and a flat red roof made of concrete and designed to withstand typhoons. The husband and wife team were standing at the open door. Weng and the other girls were behind them. The husband and wife stepped aside and the girls approached the old man. "Please, privacy," he told the employers, who stepped back without taking their eyes off the girls who were now in a huddle with *Tun* Jack. They whispered. And whispered some more. Then *Tun* Jack told the couple, "You let them go, let them resign, allow them to transfer, they won't file complaint. Guaranteed." The couple consulted with each other and then made a counter-offer: "OK, they go, but not yet, because nothing girls if they leave right away." So when could they resign, asked the old man. The couple exchanged furious whispers. Then, the wife said: one month from now. They still had to recruit replacements. *Tun* Jack told the girls that it was the best that could be done considering the circumstances. OK, the girls said. *Tun* Jack told the employers: No hard feelings OK? The couple nodded, reluctantly. Let's be friends again, the old man said.

It was an uneasy and awkward truce, but *Tun* Jack, the peacemaker, did his part by checking on the girls every night at the bar, and chatting with the employers as if nothing was the matter.

"Your hero," I told Weng. She said nothing. We were in my room. Another Friday afternoon. She was lying in bed, watching TV, the Filipino channel. I was beside her. An old Filipino movie was on.

"Where will you go once you're 'free' of your employers?" I asked, staring at the TV screen. "I heard that some of the other girls will work for other clubs." Pause. "What about you?"

"What else?"

"You're 'eloping' with the old man?"

"He says I can still work. But."

"What?"

"He says I must not work for a bar anymore."

"So?"

"He says he'll find me a new job."

"So you're—"

"You ask so many questions. As if."

"What?"

"Yes, *what* is it to you? Why do you need to know these things anyway?"

"I was just—"

"Do you think we can still do this once I'm with him?"

In matters of the heart—or my gonads—Weng was staggeringly mature although she was eight years younger than I. I was a mere blubbering adolescent in her presence.

"I uh, uh…"

"I'd turn my back on him—for you. But that will never happen. You have someone else in the P.I. And I'm just a bar girl." She said it without a trace of self-pity.

"I um, um…"

"Just shut up Benjie."

It was great advice.

36

*T*UN Jack finally agreed to meet me and talk about what he knew about Amelia Earhart. But he said he was a busy man and his only free time was in the evening.

"So you want me to drop by your house," I asked over the phone.

"No *lai*. Meet me at Hot Stuff." Weng's bar.

"What time sir?"

"Make it 7:30. Drinks on you."

Crap. "Sure thing," I replied. I would just ask for a reimbursement.

From the office, I headed to the nearest ATM, withdrew some cash and headed to Hot Stuff. The old man's Nissan Pathfinder was the only other vehicle in the parking lot.

He was also the only customer. Weng was seated with him at a table near the stage. No one was dancing, but loud music was playing. Aerosmith's "Crazy."

I sat across from Weng who was sipping her $14 lady's drink that I would have to pay for. "Hi *kuya*!" she said. *Kuya* is the Filipino term for older brother or older male relative. It also refers to total strangers who happen to be men and older than you. A Filipina will sometimes use it to, as the Americans would put it, cockblock a man they're not interested in. You're just a brother to her, nothing more.

"Hi *kuya*!" Weng said again because even in the dark I looked irritated after she called me *kuya* the first time.

"Hi *até*!" I said, which is what we call our older sister or older female relative.

Weng giggled. *Tun* Jack coughed and said, "Beer?"

"Sure," I said.

"I'll get it," Weng stood up.

"What do you think of her," the old man said, holding onto his bottle of Miller Lite.

"Who?"

"Maja."

"Not my type."

He looked at me.

"I've got bad taste, unlike you." God, what was I saying!

"Anyway," he said, still looking at me like he thought I was going to snatch something that belonged to him once he looked away.

"Here you go *kuya*!" Weng placed a bottle of Miller Lite in front of me.

"Daddy can I have another drink?" she asked. *Daddy*. I wanted to puke.

"You ask him," Jack pointed at me. "He's paying."

"*Kuya*?"

"Sure sure." I wanted to say something in Filipino to her but *that* would be the height of rudeness.

"Yey." And she proceeded to the bar to get her 14-dollar watered-down iced-tea.

I had to get what I needed from the old man before he and his girlfriend ordered more drinks.

"Sir, what do you know about Amelia Earhart?"

Tun Jack was about my height, which was 5'6", and he looked like he was in his 70s, but I learned that he was only in his early 60s. He had dark brown skin and thinning hair that used to be all gray but he had been dyeing it lately, no doubt to look "younger" to his girlfriend who could be his granddaughter.

The old man, moreover, was slim. Not even a beer belly. A government retiree, he was still active in local politics especially in election years, campaigning for his political party and candidates. Now and then, small businesses owned by foreigners would hire him as a "consultant"—a fixer, basically. The dude who could expedite the processing of papers required by many regulatory agencies.

His kids were in the states and he was a widower, but he didn't live alone in his two-story house in Chalan Kanoa, which used to be the capital town of the island. Cousins, nieces and nephews would often stay there for a day of two, and he didn't mind. Family was family, he told me, adding that Filipinos and other Asians would understand.

As for Amelia Earhart, he said it was in the 1950s when he first learned that there were local people who claimed to have seen her and her co-pilot on Saipan in the late 1930s.

"But that's just talk," I said.

"I knew the man who knew where they were buried," referring to Earhart and her navigator Fred Noonan.

"Where is that man?"

"*Matai* already." Dead.

"Great."

"But I know what he knows and I can prove it."

"How?"

"I know where the bones are."

"But I was told that the bones exhumed from the supposed gravesite turned out to be the remains of locals."

"I'm talking about the bones of the American lady and her companion."

"Why are you telling me this now? I was told that some statesiders flew to Saipan looking for her remains."

"That was a long time ago. In 1961. Yeah but they got the wrong bones. And other haoles have been here since then, but they never asked me or my friend who also knew but is now *matai*, too. They could talk to me. They talked to everyone but not me."

"Morons."

"Yah *nei*."

37

MY publisher Sam said he knew many locals, some in their 60s and 70s already, who heard about the two Americans held by the Japanese on island in the late 1930s. "It was common knowledge, according to the locals," Sam said, "but it's all hearsay without physical evidence, and that's what we're after. Clothing, photo or photos, a piece of Earhart's plane, her remains—something verifiable. A piece or pieces of the truth. Until then it's all he-said, she-said, we-said, they-said, who-knows."

Rob, who had drawn up plans for a museum and a history tour package once he found proof that Amelia did die on Saipan, told me what he had learned so far. He said he first heard it in the states from the wife of a World War

II veteran who was assigned to the island in the 1950s. Rob said a newspaper in Indiana interviewed the old lady in 1990. He showed me a photocopy—one of many he had—of the following news clipping:

BURLINGTON, Ky. — Few mysteries have intrigued the American public like the disappearance of flier Amelia Earhart. Speculation about Miss Earhart's fate surfaces in books and the media from time to time. Recently the prime-time television show Unsolved Mysteries *featured the 53-year-old puzzler. Charlotte White of Burlington, Ky., hasn't solved the puzzle of Miss Earhart's disappearance during a round-the-world flight in 1937. But Mrs. White can add a few pieces.*

Mrs. White met a man on the Pacific island of Saipan who claimed to know Miss Earhart's fate. The man, a police chief on the island, showed Mrs. White a leather flyer's jacket that he said belonged to "the lady flyer." In tropical Saipan, it's unlikely a native would wear a leather jacket at any time of year. Mrs. White lived on Saipan from 1955 to 1961 with her husband, Edward, who has since died. A retired Army master sergeant and World War II prisoner of the Germans, White worked for the CIA. "I'd heard about Amelia Earhart being missing, everybody in America had. But I never connected it with Saipan," recalled Mrs. White, now 71. "Then one day I was being driven home, and we were stopped by some people who said they were from Look *magazine, and were doing research on a story about Amelia Earhart."*

Mrs. White began asking some questions of her own, and ultimately talked with the police chief, named Gurerro [sic]. He had been on the island when it was occupied by the Japanese, before American forces captured it in 1944. "He said he remembered the flyers, and he described Miss Earhart to a T," White said. "She had curly brown hair. 'They killed her,' he said of the Japanese." Gurerro told her that Miss Earhart's plane had crashed near Saipan, apparently when it flew off course and ran out of fuel. "Her co-pilot [sic], Fred Noonan, was injured in the crash and soon died, the police chief said. He took me to Garapan, a large city [sic] which had been heavily damaged during the war, and showed me the place where he said they kept her in an underground cell. 'She was very sick,' he said."

Miss Earhart was buried within the military's postwar training ground, which is off-limits, according to Gurerro. Gurerro had the jacket hanging on a hook in his office. "He said it was the lady flyer's jacket, but he didn't say how he got it. I tried to touch it and he said, 'No Missy, don't touch.' He let me look at it, but he wouldn't let me touch it," Mrs. White said. "I have absolutely nothing to authenticate any of this. All I know is what he told me all those years ago."

The memory comes back to her from time to time, especially when someone mentions Amelia Earhart or something appears in the news or on television, such as the Unsolved Mysteries *segment. No investigator has ever contacted her since she met the* Look *magazine reporters. She didn't know anything at the time, she said. Her husband, who may have known something he never told her, admonished her not to talk about it. Edward White, who worked as a security guard after the family returned to Kentucky, died in 1989. Mrs. White would like to go back to Saipan for another look, but she isn't keen on a flight across the ocean. She had enough of that, she says, as an Army and CIA wife.*

"What if that jacket still exists?" Rob said.

"That 'Gurerro' dude," I said; "*Tun* Jack knew him."

38

THE old man and Weng—be still my beating heart—got married shortly after she and the other bar girls were allowed to resign by their erstwhile employers. I wasn't invited to the wedding which was held at the mayor's office. The reception was at a hotel restaurant, and the guests included Weng's co-workers and *Tun* Jack's friends which included some ranking government officials. I learned all this from Weng herself when I bumped into her in a supermarket where she was arranging cartons of milk on one of the shelves. Her husband got her the job. And no, she told me, no more "one last memory" with me. "Move on," she said. "I'm a married woman now." Then she looked at me as if she would never see me again.

Her old man never told me where to find Amelia Earhart's supposed bones. But he said he would talk to me again, soon.

"Is he just pulling our legs?" I asked Manny.

"When will you meet with him again?" he asked.

"He says he'll call me."

"When?"

I shrugged.

Rob also wanted to meet with *Tun* Jack.

"I'll introduce you to him," I said.

"When? Where?"

"I can't badger him, you know," I said. "He might get pissed."

"Is he still mad at you for banging his wife?"

"They weren't married yet when that happened, and she told him it never happened, and I think he wants to believe that."

"Hah."

"I just have to wait."

We were in Rob's living room. It was another relaxed Friday evening. His girlfriend, Mila, was cooking dinner in the kitchen. Rob and I were drinking canned Miller Lite, watching CNN while waiting for a friend of his, another statesider who had been living on Saipan for several years now. His name was Fred and he was a teacher in a private school. His girlfriend Jing was Filipina, a waitress who was Mila's friend.

Fred was in his early 40s, twice divorced, tall and lanky with a matching long face, clean-shaven with thick gray hair. "Dude," he said to Rob before looking at me and nodding. "Hey," he said. "Hey," I said. "Fred, Benjie, Benjie, Fred," Rob said. "The reporter dude," Fred said. "Honey," he told his girlfriend, Jing; "don't say anything bad about me to this guy." We all laughed. Jing handed the roasted chicken wrapped in aluminum foil to Rob while Fred went straight to the refrigerator to put his 12 cans of Budweiser on ice.

Fred and Rob were into spelunking and digging up World War II-era artifacts in the jungles: battered U.S. and Japanese canteens, bullets, old soda bottles, bayonets and skulls. Shouldn't they turn over their finds to the local museum? I asked Rob while, Hamlet-like, he gazed at a skull which he held on his right palm. We were having a drink in his living room.

"Sure, I'll do that," he said. "Soon. Mila hates this stuff."

"I wonder why."

Like Rob, Fred believed that he knew what happened to Amelia Earhart. Unlike Rob, however, Fred insisted that after Amelia was captured by the Japanese, she was interned in Japan and, after the war, returned to the states where she assumed a new identity in New Jersey.

"That's nuts," Rob said. They argued about it every time they see each other.

"Mrs. Irene Bolam."

"Who?" I asked.

"Why do you have to ask." Rob groaned.

"A.k.a. Amelia Earhart."

"What?"

Rob groaned again.

"Mrs. Irene Bolam became Amelia's new identity. She didn't want to be Amelia anymore."

Fred then asked me: "What about you. What do you think really happened to her?"

"Well," I said, "based on what I've read so far, her plane probably crash-landed in the ocean, killing her and Noonan, and their plane sank which is why nobody could find it or their remains."

Rob and Fred looked at each other and laughed.

39

O

N May 27, 1960, the *San Mateo Times* in California ran the following banner story with the headline: SAN MATEAN SAYS JAPANESE EXECUTED AMELIA EARHART. According to the news story: "A San Mateo woman who may have been one of the last to see Amelia Earhart alive, says that the famed aviatrix was executed by a Japanese firing squad even while the U.S. Navy was spending $4,000,000 in a futile search for the missing flier and her navigator, Fred Noonan. Mrs. Josephine Blanco Akiyama... has identified pictures of Amelia as the 'American lady pilot' she saw taken into custody on the fortress island of Saipan in July, 1937. The woman flier was accompanied by a man, she said, an American also dressed in aviator's garb."

And then there's *Daughter of the Sky: The Story of Amelia Earhart,* a book written by Capt. Paul Briand Jr., an assistant English professor at the Air Force Academy, published in 1960:

In the summer of 1937 Josephine was riding her bicycle toward Tanapag Harbor. She was taking her Japanese brother-in-law, J.Y. Matsumoto, his lunch, and was hurrying along because it was nearly twelve o'clock... Josephine had a special pass to the Japanese military area near the harbor. Not even Japanese civilians were admitted to the area unless they carried the proper credentials. The young girl rode up to the gate, stopped her bicycle, and presented her pass. The guard allowed her into the restricted area. On the way to meet her brother-in-law, Josephine heard an airplane flying overhead. She looked up and saw a silver two-engine plane. The plane seemed to be in trouble, for it came down low, headed out into the harbor, and belly-landed on the water. It was not until she met her brother-in-law that Josephine discovered whom it was that had crash-landed in the harbor. "The American woman," everyone was saying, greatly excited. "Come and see the American woman." Josephine and her brother-in-law joined the knot of people who gathered to watch. She saw the American woman standing next to a tall man wearing a short-sleeved sports shirt, and was surprised because the woman was not dressed as a woman usually dressed. Instead of a dress, the American woman wore a man's shirt and trousers; and instead of long hair, she wore her hair cut short, like a man. The faces of the man and woman were white and drawn, as if they were sick.

According to Briand, "Josephine identified photos of Earhart and Noonan as absolutely being the same pair she saw on Saipan in 1937."

Hearsay upon hearsay, I told Rob.

"Are there proofs that these accounts are not true?" Rob asked.

Fred said it was also an "established fact" that Earhart and Noonan landed in the Marshalls Islands from where they were taken by the Japanese to Saipan.

"And why should islanders on Saipan and the Marshalls claim that they saw Earhart and Noonan?" Rob asked.

"I don't know," I said.

"They have absolutely nothing to gain from saying that," Fred said.

"And in the case of the witnesses on Saipan," Rob said, "they recounted their stories to priests. And we know how devout they were in those days. You simply didn't lie to your priest, especially about something that didn't concern you."

"So where's the physical, solid evidence to prove it?"

"When do I get to meet old man Jack?" Rob asked.

40

*T*UN Jack never gave me his phone number. "I'll call you; don't call me." And since "settling down" with a wife who was the same age as one of his granddaughters, I could no longer find him in any bar on island. He never told me where he lived. When I went to see Weng at the supermarket where she worked, she told me to stop bothering her and that her *husband*—she said it like it was a profanity directed against me—her husband told me he would call me, so I should believe him because he was a man of his word.

"What's with all this goddamn suspense Benjie?" Sam asked me at the office.

"Maybe the old man's still mad at you," Manny said.

"I thought you fixed that already," Sam said.

"I thought I did," I said.

"So?"

"I was told to wait."

"Man."

Tun Jack did call, later that day, to tell me that he had forgotten.

"Forgot what sir?" I asked.

"Where the bones are."

"Where were they supposed to be?"

"Good question."

"*Tun* Jack."

"Yes *lai*."

"With all due respect…"

"Yes."

"Are you shitting me?"

"*Lanya.* Don't talk to me like that."

"I'm sorry sir, but…"

"Just give me time *lai*…"

"Can I be of any assistance?"

"I think you've been assisting too much already."

Crap. He still hated me.

"I could help you look for whatever it is you're looking for." I pretended not to get his drift.

"The problem," he said, "is that they're not where they're supposed to be."

41

I GRIEVED over losing Weng. I never had her, true, but I still managed to lose her. I was so sad at times that even my editor, Manny, noticed. Especially because he saw me sulking, again, at my desk, just staring at my Mac and its blinking cursor.

"Bring her over," he said. It was lunch time, and we were the only ones left in the newsroom. Manny was waiting for his partner to pick him up. I wasn't hungry yet.

"Your girlfriend in Manila," Manny said.

"Huh?"

"You told me she's a nurse."

"Yeah."

"Ask around. One of the private clinics here, for sure, needs a nurse or a healthcare provider."

I said nothing.

"Bring her over as a tourist. Maybe she'll like it here."

I still said nothing.

"Either that or you'll be more miserable than you already are."

Indisputable.

"I don't know about you, but I found it hard to sleep alone." Manny paused. "It'll solve a lot of things."

"What?"

"Your girlfriend here with you on island."

I said nothing.

"I'm of course assuming you still want her."

"Of course I do…"

"There you…"

"…I think."

"…go. Wait, what?"

"No, I…"

"Whatever. Bring her over. Then you'll find out. Talk to her about it. Plan it now. Have something to look forward to. Just stop moping like a teenager turned down in public by his crush."

I did somewhat miss Sweet.

"Yes! Yes! Yes!" she screamed on the phone that night, when I called her. She was at the hospital. She didn't care. "Did he just propose?" I heard someone said in the background.

"I thought you'd never ask! When? When? When?"

"Uh, I guess as soon as you…"

"Yes! Yes! Yes!"

First, we had to set a date. I was thinking of two or three months down the road, but Sweet said, Why not next month? She could file a notice of leave right away. I would make all the flight arrangements, of course. As for her parents, she would tell them that she would go on an all-expense-paid job-hunting trip. I would often visit Sweet at their home so her parents knew and probably even liked me. They had also met my mother at our home on the feast day of our village patron saint. Sweet brought them along—it was her idea—to, more or less, "formalize" our relationship, and basically to assure her parents that even though we were most likely and sadly indulging in pre-marital coitus, we were on the pathway to matrimonial respectability. But her parents said a month on a faraway island with me was too much. (Too much what?) She told them that she would have her own room, but they didn't buy it. Two weeks tops, her parents finally said because Sweet kept bugging them.

"Tell her not to bring a lot of stuff," Manny told me. "Customs is suspicious of young 'tourists' from Manila."

"Ice?" I asked, referring to what we called shabu back home. Crystal methamphetamine. For me, the world's most ridiculous illegal drug. I don't care if you're the coolest man in the world, you'll look like a loser if you smoke it.

"Did you hear," Manny said, "about the young 'mom' from Manila who had an infant with her on the plane?"

"No."

"During the flight, she asked for coffee. Stewardess gave it to her. Hot coffee. Some of it accidentally spilled on the 'baby.' Baby didn't cry."

"Crap."

"So the stewardess reported it to the captain who advised immigration about it."

"They searched the baby."

"Baby'd been dead for days. Sewn up. Inside were plastic bags of 'ice' with a street value of hundreds of thousands of dollars."

"Sweet has to travel light."

"Make sure you tell her."

42

SWEET said she told the Saipan immigration officer that I, her boyfriend, was picking her up. The officer recognized my name. "The reporter?" he asked Sweet. "Yes sir." The customs officer who checked her one and only piece of luggage looked at the books it contained and said, "You gonna read all that?" Sweet said they belonged to her boyfriend, the reporter. No, the island's immigration and customs officers did not find reporters impressive at all. But they considered us the least likely to use a mule in smuggling drugs.

Sweet was soon out of the airport and into my arms. I did miss her: her presence—the feel of her skin, her scent. It was like embracing Manila, or a non-polluted, softer and pleasant-looking version of it.

"I don't like your long hair," she said. I didn't say anything. Weng liked it.

Sweet would stay in my room at the barracks. I had sought the boss's permission, of course, assuring him that we would move out if Sweet and I ever decided to get married. Sam said OK.

And while on island Sweet would look for a job.

"Raise a family here," Noel told. "Your kids will have U.S. passports. They'll get to see Disneyland in Anaheim."

We laughed. Noel's girlfriend on island was pregnant again, less than a year after she gave birth.

"You and your sweetheart should join the bowling league or volunteer for the Red Cross or something," Manny advised Noel. "You have way too much time on your hands."

Noel was also trying to "work things out" with his wife in the P.I.

"That guy has to move on," Manny told me, referring to Noel. "He, we, can't have it both ways. But I—no one—can tell him what to do with his personal life. So in your case, I suggest that you bring your girlfriend along when you leave for work and do not leave her at the barracks. She'll end up chatting with the loudmouths there who may eventually say something you don't want your girlfriend to know."

The loudmouths were the wives of some of our older co-employees. There were three of them, the yappers we called them, and they were already in their late 30s or early 40s. They used to be employees, too, on island: waitresses or hotel housekeepers, but after giving birth to their children, they decided to be full-time housewives—either that or they had to get babysitters. When their kids started going to school, they became babysitters themselves, looking after the babies of their husbands' co-workers or friends who would bring the infants to the barracks and pick them up after 5 p.m. each working day.

I was pretty sure that no one among these blabbermouths saw me bring Weng to my unit. But you could never really know for sure—until you pissed them off, and then you'd know, said Manny, who was speaking from experience.

From the airport, I brought Sweet to the La Fiesta Mall in San Roque where we had dinner in a Japanese restaurant. Sweet was impressed. "This is so expensive back home!" she said, looking at the food I had ordered which included crunchy shrimp tempura roll and a gorgeous variety of sushi. After dinner, we drove to the Hotel Nikko, which was across from the mall, for some cocktails near the beach.

"So fabulous," Sweet said. "So nice. It's like we're rich already!" Back home, only the rich could afford to go to a similar beach resort in the central Philippines.

"And so many Japanese and Filipinos!" she added.

"The Japanese are the tourists and we're the help."

"Sure beats working in Manila." And its noise, air-pollution, low-paying jobs, the traffic, the pickpockets, snatchers and robbers—the humanity.

I was starting *not* to miss any of them.

Sweet arrived on a Saturday, late afternoon. From Hotel Nikko I brought her to one of the small hotels in Garapan where we checked in and spent the night.

On the following day, we drove around the island with Sweet oohing and aahing a lot. "It's like we're in a province," she said; "a very clean province." And then we had lunch at one of the hotels down south—the sheer amount of food and the glorious buffet spread that included salads, appetizers, desserts and bottomless drinks likewise impressed her.

"Are you sure we're not rich yet?" she asked, giggling.

Manny gave me the day off—I had filed my stories on Friday anyway—so Sweet and I were tourists all day, going to one scenic spot after another. We also dropped by at Rob's place—I phoned first, of course—and Sweet blushed repeatedly every time Rob praised her "cuteness." Rob had been drinking and his girlfriend wasn't around.

"He's nice," Sweet told me in the car later.

"He's an alcoholic."

It was already early in the evening when I brought Sweet to our barracks. The guys were at one table—except for Noel who was probably in his unit, babysitting his kid—and they were drinking Filipino gin and soda while having a barbecue. As for the ladies, and I use the term loosely, they were playing cards at another table. Everyone was looking at us as we walked toward my room.

"Benjie!" someone who was already drunk said.

I just smiled and nodded my head.

"Introduce us to your sweetie-pie!" one of the women said.

I was still smiling.

"Hi!" Sweet said, beaming, waving to them. She was always…friendly.

"Hi!" the denizens of the barracks said in unison.

"Come join us!" one of them added.

"Benjie she's so pretty!" another drunk said.

"She still has to unpack," I said. "But we'll join you guys in a few."

"Be sure ha." Laughter.

"Not yet the loving-loving ha." More laughter.

Sweet was still smiling. I was fake-smiling and it hurt.

"You look tired hon," she said.

"I'm beat, but they'll keep hollering at us if we don't come out."

So we did join my gambling and/or drinking fellow workers. It was like a press conference. Everyone asked her questions. Others made loud comments, as if they were watching a TV talk show.

"Benjie's so lucky!"

"He'll be luckier soon."

I was smiling, painfully, as I wondered if there was really no one among my neighbors who knew about me and Weng. I brought her to the barracks at least once a week.

Of course, if someone did know, he or she would not spill it there and then. No, not yet. He or she had to be pretty pissed at me before they would say something about it. So I had to be nice to everyone, all the time.

I groaned.

"Hon?" Sweet asked. "You OK?"

"Yeah," I lied. "Trying to stifle a yawn."

"Benjie really missed you a lot," one of the drunks said.

Sweet chuckled.

"He was always talking about you," another said.

"Sometimes we could even hear him crying."

I no longer loved the masses.

43

ND of course, Sweet and I had to stumble into Weng and *Tun* Jack at the swanky duty-free shop in Garapan. Weng was checking out one of the brand-name purses—Prada, Louis Vuitton, Chanel, Burberry, Coach—that cost hundreds if not thousands of dollars. *Tun* Jack looked bored and walked toward to the counter where the men's wallets were. He had his back turned to Weng who was blabbing about how beautiful the purses were at the exact moment when Sweet and I were beside Weng because Sweet, too, wanted to look at the purses.

"What about this one daddy?" Weng turned around, holding a lavender handbag, staring at me looking at her.

She blushed. "*Ay* sorry," she said, looking at Sweet who was holding my hand, her eyes on the purses. "Where is that old man," Weng said as he she hurriedly walked to where *Tun* Jack was. I didn't want to look at him. I didn't want to talk to him right there and then under extremely awkward circumstances.

Naturally, he saw me, and said, *"Hafa* Benjie. *Mauleg'ka?"*

"Hi sir. I'm good."

He looked at Sweet who was still looking at the purses. Weng was trying to look at something else. I had to look at *Tun* Jack.

"Si Mrs.?" he asked. Sweet turned around. "Very pretty," he added.

"Thank you," Sweet said, still pleased to hear it, even though she heard it a lot.

"My girlfriend, Sweet," I said. They shook hands.

"This is my wife," he said. Weng now had no choice but to look at me and Sweet. *"Si* Rowena," *Tun* Jack said.

"Hi!"

"Hello!"

"We're friends of Benjie," *Tun* Jack said. I was quite sure I winced. Weng was still smiling, as if to a rabid dog and hoping it would not bite her.

"So you're going to work here, too?" *Tun* Jack asked Sweet. Now and then, I was stealing glances at Weng. Then I saw her stealing a glance at me.

"Benjie," the old man said, smiling, looking at Sweet who was also smiling like a seasoned politician. "I'll give you a call tomorrow OK? About that thing." He seemed to be, finally, pleased with me.

"All right," I said. Weng, smiling half-heartedly, was looking at Sweet.

The next day, Weng phoned me at the office. Sweet was with Manny's wife, who took the day off so she and Sweet could drive around the island.

"Hello," Weng said, as if replying to a question I haven't asked yet.

"Miss you," I said.

"Hmmmp."

"I do."

"She's pretty."

"Where are you?"

"Where is she?"

"Not here. Where is he?

"He went out. I think he's going to your office."

"I miss you."

"So you'll shack up with her?"

"If she finds work."

"Will you marry her?"

"I guess."

"Hmmmp."

"You miss me?"

Before she could answer, someone tapped me on my shoulder. I looked around and it was Weng's husband, smiling at me.

"Gotta go," I said to his wife and hung up. I was pretty sure my face was red as a baboon's ass.

"You OK?" *Tun* Jack said. "I seemed to have interrupted you."

"Yes, no," I said as I stood up patting the pockets of my pants as if I had forgotten something or was looking for it. I was trying to avoid looking at the old man. "My ballpen," I said.

"There," *Tun* Jack said, pointing to it there on the keyboard in front of me.

"Oh yeah," I said as I put the ballpen in my shirt pocket. I could sense how hot my cheeks and ears were.

I brought him to the office of my publisher, Sam, who was having a meeting with my editor, Manny.

After exchanging pleasantries with Sam and Manny, *Tun* Jack and Sam talked about the good ol' days, and the people they both knew, until Sam, finally, mentioned Amelia Earhart.

"Wouldn't it be great for Saipan if we could prove to the world that she was here—that this was the last piece of God's good earth that she ever saw?"

Tun Jack agreed. "Plenty people in the Marshalls and here said they saw or heard about her being brought here. And I think we have evidence."

"Gravesite?" Manny asked.

"I'm not sure about that anymore. I thought there were bones, but I think they're just photos," *Tun* Jack said.

"Oh," Sam said.

"The lady posing with Japanese officers. And photo of her plane, too."

"Did you see them yourself, these photos?" Manny asked.

"I think I did when I was a kid. I never really gave those photos much thought. I was a kid. But as I grew older, now and then haoles would arrive from the states and snoop around, asking questions about that lady. No one ever asked me, as I've told Benjie here."

"Even U.S. veterans who saw action here heard about Amelia," Sam said.

"So do you have them, the photos?" Manny asked.

"*Lanya*, that's the problem *lai*."

"You lost them?" I asked.

"I can't find them anymore."

"Like the bones?" I asked.

Tun Jack looked at me. "I'm not fooling around."

"Do you want to get paid for whatever you have?" Sam asked. "We can't give you money, but once we run the story, I guarantee you that the big shots in the U.S. media will try to outbid each other in getting those photos from you."

"That's nice to know Sam, and I knew where they were, but when I looked again, they were no longer there. And now I wonder, were they ever there?"

44

HEN Sweet and I visited Rob at his place, he showed me the following Xeroxed copy of a clipping he had recently obtained, through a friend, in the states. It was from *The Berkshire County Eagle* in Pittsfield, Massachusetts and was published on July 12, 1944:

SAIPAN, July 8 (INS) — The mystery of what happened to Amelia Earhart, famous American aviatrix, popped up again today—this time on Saipan. The discovery of an album filled with Amelia Earhart pictures here on this battle-torn island revived the search for an answer to the seven-year mystery of the fate of America's number one woman flier. Some marines reported finding the album filled with pictures of Amelia Earhart clothed in sport togs. There were no other pictures in the album."

"These could be the photos *Tun* Jack was talking about," I said.

"You think?!" Rob said, scoffing; and then he smiled at Sweet.

"Well, he said he lost them."

"First he said there were bones."

"Or maybe he misplaced them."

"The bones?"

"The photos. He said he's looking for them."

"Sure. Does he need help? I can help."

"I'll ask."

"You said you'll introduce me to the old man."

"I will."

"You know," he turned to Sweet. "Not only island people said they saw or heard about Amelia's presence here. U.S. soldiers too."

"Really," Sweet said. I was pretty sure she didn't know what Rob was talking about, but she was flattered by all the attention she was getting from him. Mila, Rob's girlfriend, wasn't around. It had been quite some time since I last saw her with him, but I never asked Rob about it.

"There was this platoon sergeant," Rob said, "who interrogated a Japanese prisoner, and the sergeant said the prisoner had a photo of Amelia standing near Japanese aircraft on an airfield. The sergeant said the photo was sent up the chain of command, and according to the Japanese, the woman was taken prisoner along with her companion, a dude, and both of them were executed by the Japanese."

Rob said he had been corresponding with the author of a famous book published in the 1960s about Earhart's disappearance—the author believed that she was brought to Saipan by the Japanese. A Marine told the author that during the U.S. invasion of the island, "he saw a photo of Earhart with a Japanese officer that he believed was taken on Saipan." He said "he was clearing a house of booby traps near a graveyard when the picture was found tacked to a wall." The photo "showed Amelia standing in an open field with a Japanese soldier wearing some kind of combat or fatigue cap with a single star in its center."

According to Rob, a Seabee on island in 1945 said the local people told him how the Japanese had boasted before the war about capturing "some white people" who were brought to the island and "buried near a native cemetery."

And then there's the Marine colonel "who came into possession of photographs in Japan in 1945 that showed Earhart in Japanese custody." He said "he turned them over to [General Douglas] MacArthur's Intelligence Headquarters."

Another Marine claimed that he saw the photographs: "There were several Japanese officers with her," the Marine said, "and she certainly looked in good health.... The one picture I do recall to mind was one where Fred [Noonan] was standing sort of behind a Japanese officer to his right, and next was Amelia and then two more Japanese officers. There were other pictures of her and an officer alone and she was in sort of a fly jacket—and half a dozen others I don't remember. All were taken outdoors— no buildings in sight. Trees in background. Fred appeared much taller than Japanese. I wish I had been able to get one of those pictures. When leaving Hawaii to come back to the mainland, we were told to get rid of the souvenirs because we would have to pay a duty. We threw tons of stuff away...."

"There's just too much smoke man," Rob said. "There's gotta' be fire." He smiled at Sweet, as if he had just won an argument with her boyfriend.

I said: " 'For those who do not believe, no explanation is possible. For those who believe, no explanation is necessary.' Who said that again?"

"Party pooper," Rob said.

45

I FINALLY persuaded *Tun* Jack to meet with Rob, but the old man said it had to be in the evening, and that he wanted to check out a new karaoke bar in downtown Garapan. I couldn't resist it. "Your wife's OK that you're going out at night?" "No *lai*. She's coming with me." Sweet, of course, would tag along. Her departure date was only a few days away, and she was usually with me, and if not, she was with Manny's wife. I still didn't think that it was a good idea to leave her alone at the barracks with the gossipmongers.

Rob was already at the club when Sweet and I arrived before 8 in the evening, a weekday. We were the first customers. Rob was alone.

"Where's Mila?" I asked. He shrugged his shoulders and gave Sweet, ever smiling, a peck on her left cheek.

The karaoke bar was called Key of G, and it was on the road closest to the cluster of hotels in Garapan. There were strip and karaoke bars one after another and across from each other like a mini-version of Ermita back home but with not-so-seedy establishments and better looking young girls outside in short, tight dresses and high heels, saying hi to passersby who were mostly Japanese.

Sweet marveled at the sight of these ladies who were more or less her age. "Sexy," she said to no one in particular. Then she told me, "Have you ever been in a bar before?"

"Of course not," I said and technically I wasn't lying. I had not been in any of the girlie bars on that street until that night.

At Key of G our group sat on two sofas facing each other with a glass coffee table in the middle. Weng looked so…nice. Sweet was wearing a black blouse and jeans and looked fine as usual. Weng wore jeans shorts, a brown belt and a dark blue sleeveless shirt. She rocked her outfit.

"Hi!" Sweet greeted Weng.

"Hi!" Weng replied smiling modestly, once again avoiding looking at me, and knowing I was looking at her.

I had already introduced Rob to the old man, and the two were already talking to each other. We had also ordered drinks and the girls were already looking at the playlist to choose their karaoke songs.

Top government officials were known to hang out at Key of G which is owned by a local businessman married to a Filipina. The waitresses were all slim and long-haired, in their late teens to early 20s, very friendly, especially to Rob who, unlike me and *Tun* Jack, didn't bring his lady friend along.

Rob, however, was all business, and he and *Tun* Jack were exchanging notes about what they knew about the stories regarding Amelia Earhart's captivity on Saipan. I was, however, more interested in the guarded conversation between Weng and Sweet.

"How long have you been on island?" Sweet asked Weng.

"Almost two years," Weng replied as she sipped from her tall glass of iced tea. "What about you?" she asked Sweet. "You're staying?"

"I've got to exit. But this new clinic wants to hire me, so I'll be back."

"Oh how nice."

"What about you. Where do you work?"

"I used to work at a bar. Now I work at a store."

"That's good."

"Yeah. Better than doing nothing."

They chuckled like politicians. Then they took turns singing songs.

"Benjie." Rob tapped my shoulder. "Jack here was telling me about old local folks who, before the war, heard talk about Amelia's plane which they said was still on island at the time of the invasion."

"So what happened to it?"

"According to a U.S. pilot, he saw it in a hangar in As Lito. He said several others saw the aircraft too. But there were still Japanese snipers in the area so they couldn't get closer. He said the following day the plane was gone."

46

FTER two weeks on Saipan, Sweet went back to Manila where she would wait for up to three months for the processing of her official documents that would be sent to her by FedEx before she could fly back to the island, this time as a nurse at a recently opened private clinic that catered primarily to guest workers. We, guest workers, were required to undergo annual health check-ups. Our employers were responsible for our healthcare.

"I'm pretty sure," Rob said, "that the P.I. would be way better off if you dudes that left the country would go back and make a difference."

"That's what the Native Americans told the Pilgrims," I said, "who didn't listen."

"Ha-ha," Rob said.

"The fact that we're not there is already making a big difference for the economy," Manny replied. The three of us were at Rob's place. He wanted to meet Manny who was "free" on that Friday night. We were in Rob's living room, drinking Miller Lite and eating microwaved popcorn. CNN was on the TV like background music. Mila was not around. Rob wasn't saying anything about her and I didn't think I should pry into whatever was happening—or not happening—between them.

"You bright guys," Rob was saying, "should be back there…"

"To be as miserable as the rest?" asked Manny.

"Organize man! Agitate! Reach out!"

"We wish it was easier than that," Manny said.

"What do you mean?" I asked. I still believed that all we needed back home was good leadership—selfless, dedicated, intelligent men and women who knew where to find the right buttons at the right time to make things happen.

"It's so hard to change ourselves for the better," Manny said, "yet we believe we can change the mindset and habits of millions of other people—of an entire country. A made-up country like the Philippines and its seven thousand islands, over 80 dialects, its buffet table of cultures…"

"Whoa," Rob said.

I chuckled. Manny was usually a man of few words. But it was obvious that he had thought long and hard about what he was saying that night. He was also on his fourth can of Miller Lite.

"We're in Asia but we're not Asians," he added.

"Surely there are reformists there that can inspire," Rob said.

"If highly intelligent leaders were all that were needed to unleash progress back home then we should be like Japan now or South Korea or Taiwan."

"Really."

"We've been electing highly educated politicians since the American era. We allowed Marcos, a political genius surrounded by other geniuses, to acquire absolute power and run the country based on his blueprint for a supposed New Society. And what was the result? More of the same goddamn disaster. No wonder voters back home now prefer to elect actors and actresses. At least they're entertaining."

"What are you saying man?" Rob asked.

"Culture is destiny."

"And what is your culture?"

"The culture of short-cuts, of getting the right connections, of mediocrity in the land of the fee, home of the bribe."

"Not everyone is like that." I had to protest.

"Of course not. I'm speaking generally."

"And there are many Filipinos who have done well for themselves abroad," Rob said.

"That's the thing. You put the Filipino in a civilized nation where there is the rule of law, and he'll be law-abiding. You know one of the first things I noticed about the Pinoys here when I first arrived years ago?" Manny asked me. Without waiting for my reply, he said, "We were on the beach, drinking. There was another group of Filipinos at a nearby pavilion. They were construction workers, I was told. They were loud and they were drunk. But when it was their time to leave, each and every one of them picked up their empty beer cans and other trash and they put all in these big trash bags and into the garbage cans donated by Filipino community groups. I mean, can you imagine them, us, doing that back home where rich people in their SUVs dispose of their litter while driving on highways. We brag about our habit of daily showers…"

"That's something to brag about?" Rob chuckled.

"…but we throw trash anywhere."

"So how do you explain that?"

"We were a colony for over 400 years," I said; "that totally screwed us up. It's their fault, the Spaniards and the Yankees. No offense Rob."

"None taken."

" 'Our ills we owe to ourselves alone, so let us blame no one,' " Manny said, quoting a character from Jose Rizal's 1891 novel, *El Filibusterismo*. "[W]hy grant them liberty? With Spain or without Spain they would always be the same, and perhaps worse! Why independence, if the slaves of today will be the tyrants of tomorrow? And that they will be such is not to be doubted, for he who submits to tyranny loves it."

"You memorized all that?" I asked.

"I think I've read the English translation of that book more than 20 times."

"Why?" I asked.

Rob laughed.

Manny sighed. "Doesn't matter."

"Have you given up on the P.I.?" Rob asked.

"Or maybe it has given up on me," Manny said. "Our country is like one big class of sixth graders with no teacher or adult supervision."

"To Amelia Earhart!" Rob said, raising his ninth or tenth can of beer.

47

I EVENTUALLY realized that *Tun* Jack had a finger in many of the island's proverbial pies. He was, I learned, a political foot soldier who rose through the ranks and was now considered an all-round "fixer." He knew everyone who should be known in the local government which made him valuable to business interests, especially foreign ones. He knew, of course, the patriarchs and the matriarchs of the local families. He was the head-counter in an election year. It was his job to know who would vote for what candidate. He was considered loyal to his political party, and even the leaders of the other party appreciated his skills and professionalism, and wished they were employed on their behalf. He himself had never held high positions in government which he didn't want anyway. He preferred good old fashioned sinecures.

"Everything I know about politics," Senator Guzman once told me, "I learned from the old man."

"And what do you now know senator?"

"Off the record OK. Here's what I've learned: don't talk too much (especially to reporters); listen, really listen and not just wait to butt in again during a conversation; understand where the other guy is coming from—where he stands depends on where he sits; never pick a fight unless you have to, and if you have to, make sure you win, but don't burn bridges; and never get mad."

I smiled.

"*Lanya*, the one thing I still don't know how to do is stay away from reporters."

I once told *Tun* Jack that I wanted to write a feature story about him and his interesting life.

"Why the hell would you do that *lai*?" was his reply.

Of course. Why would he give the game away? He wasn't supposed to exist. In a representative democracy, the people ruled through their elected officials, and it did not involve politicking politicians and their fixers and gofers.

"These young locals today," *Tun* Jack told me, "don't know how lucky they are."

"What do you mean?" I asked.

"Everything's served to them on a silver platter, as the haoles would put it. They don't know how different life was when their grandparents were their age."

"How was it?"

"We lived on a small rock. That was it."

He showed me an old copy of a news magazine published by statesiders during the Trust Territory era. The year was 1969. Among the articles was a guide to Saipan beaches. There were no good roads on the island back then, *Tun* Jack told me.

"Many of the beaches were not accessible," he said. "There were trees and grass everywhere. My sisters didn't even learn how to swim! And they were born on a small island!"

The magazine also featured a poem titled "Poverty Is" written by a young man from Saipan.

"He's describing what life was back in the day. The kids today think it was the golden age or something."

"Poverty," says the poem, "is getting married at 23, earning 50 cents an hour. This includes not having a house."

Poverty is you expect to live with your mother-in-law, with 4 kids.

Poverty is going to your neighbor to wash your clothes, clothes you have worn several days to work.

Poverty is what you saw at your neighbors.

Poverty is finding the cupboard empty.

Poverty is what you put on the table for your family's meal, of nine.

Poverty is looking at your wife's rosy cheeks turning pale.

Poverty is owning a house built by materials from crates as old as World War II halfway eaten by termites and weather-beaten, cracked.

Poverty is having diseases destroying breadfruit and coconut trees all over the place.

Poverty is planting crops on barren soil.

Poverty's your home demolished, losing your clothes, finding broken dishes, soaked rice sacks and broken chairs, after each typhoon.

Poverty is living with 6 people in an 8' x 16' shack for three months, with a baby 60 days old.

Poverty is picking up pieces and putting them together.

Poverty is seeing choice land rotting away that no one can do anything with.

Poverty is trying to live as the Americans taught you.

Poverty is dressed with creases on your worn trousers, faded and mended shirt on your back.

Poverty is seeing them wear earrings, wrist watches, carrying cameras.

Poverty is seeing them wearing dark glasses, laughing.

Poverty is seeing them live comfortable, in concrete houses.

Poverty is seeing mowed lawns with gay colored flowers, overgrown grass in my yard instead.

Poverty is seeing air-conditioners protruding at each wall.

Poverty is not washing your dishes with warm water, with soap.

Poverty is getting wet going to the bathroom.

Poverty is taking a shower with a trickle for water, the water running red from corrosions in the pipes, 20 years old.

Poverty is not having huge glass picture windows to watch scenery and the ship docking

Poverty is seeing your darling children, with their tummys growing bigger from worms.

Poverty is paying or not being able to pay the hospital bills.

Poverty is getting sick.

Poverty is catching the flu and the only medicine you get is aspirin tablets.

Poverty is not having rice on the table, $7 or more for a 50 pound bag.

Poverty is seeing your children attending classes at school, under army tents.

Poverty is seeing your island overgrown with tangantangan trees.

Poverty is water pipelines knocked out.

Poverty is getting surplus equipment, excess needs of other federal agencies.

Poverty is having holes on the roads.

Poverty is seeing a bulldozer on the road shoulder, for a week.

Poverty is when it rains the roads are flooded.

Poverty is politics.

Poverty is unequal representation, the Micronesian Pay Scale.

And Poverty is when you are face to face sitting down at the table, mumbling, "Bless us O Lord, and these thy gifts ..."

48

MY publisher, Sam, said that in the good old days, the local economy was basically the Trust Territory government the headquarters of which were on Saipan. He said the airport was a tin shack and an unlighted runway. "There was one airplane a day and one cargo ship a month," he added. "There wasn't anything here. But there were three stores that sold food. You had to visit each one of them to complete a shopping list. The fire department was a red Jeep with a garden hose. If you wanted to make an overseas call, you had to go to the RCA booth in Susupe and make that call. There were no recreation craft in the lagoon. We had one radio station and black and white television station that came on about 7 and was off by 11:30. I'm talking about the early 1970s. It seemed like the early 1950s."

Tun Jack said most local people wanted development—they wanted American consumer products; they wanted to go to the states and receive an American education at American schools.

"The haoles thought we were crazy to want those things."

"Many of them were pro-Americans back then," Sam said, referring to the locals. "There was this local official, Joe, who appeared before a congressional hearing in D.C. Congress was still deliberating on whether to approve the Covenant with the islands that would make them part of the U.S. Joe sang 'God Bless America' during one of the hearings. There wasn't a dry eye in the place. 'Oh it's so nice,' one of the ladies on the House committee said, wiping her tears away. Elsewhere around the world, we were getting our butts kicked, in Vietnam especially. But here was Joe singing, with feeling, 'While the storm clouds gather far across the sea,/ Let us swear allegiance to a land that's free,/ Let us all be grateful for a land so fair.' "

"One haole official told me," Tun Jack said, " 'the transistor radio will ruin your island.' But we had nothing. How could you ruin nothing? And you can't stop people wanting what they see other people have. But these haoles who had washing machines and dryers and everything else would tell us, 'You have a marvelous climate and you've got the trade winds, you can dry your clothes outside.' I laughed in their faces."

Sam said: "Most of the statesiders who were here at that time, present company included, wanted the island as it was: a rock covered with trees. We found the horrible roads quaint. It was as if we were on a dried-up river. The backwardness of it all was what we, coming from Nixon's America, wanted."

"All we wanted was a better life, for us and our children, and their children," *Tun* Jack said.

"We thought they already had a good life," Sam said.

"And then life got better. Suddenly we had more money. Good roads, homes made of concrete. Hotels and restaurants and lots of cars, and our kids and grandkids could now get a college education in the states..."

"Ask them now if they're happy."

"Now we complain of other things."

My editor Manny put it this way: "Adam and Eve in the Garden of Eden. They had everything. There was no suffering. No poverty. No hunger. No greed. No need for welfare. No crime. No violence. Eternal life! Government was literally divine. God was in charge and not just His self-proclaimed messengers or prophets. God Himself governed and was on call 24/7. He only had one rule. Don't eat the forbidden fruit. That was all. Easy to remember. Easy to follow. Adam and Eve had what we their descendants could only dream about. So what did Adam and Eve do? They wanted more. Paradise wasn't enough. They wanted to be like God. We were already defective then, and I'm quite sure we're still pretty much messed up today, yet we still believe we can do a better job than God."

49

MANNY believed that *Tun* Jack had the Amelia Earhart evidence all this time, but for some reason, he didn't want to share it with us—yet. "He'd give it to us when there's a need for him to give it to us," Manny said. "Unless you piss him off again."

"I'm not doing anything to piss him off," I said, and it was true. Sure, now and then, Weng would call and we would talk, but that was all. And Sweet was scheduled to return to the island, a fact that I usually mention to the old man every time we meet at the legislative building.

"Something's cooking," Senator Guzman told me in the parking lot. It was around 9 in the morning, and I had just arrived, but he was already leaving. "I'm still not sure if I want to be part of it," he added, as got into his dark blue Nissan Pathfinder.

"What?" I asked.

"Can't say anything now. But it doesn't smell good."

"What?"

"Don't tell them you saw me."

Them were the other members of the Senate leadership who were in the Senate president's conference room.

Every day, I would drop into the Senate president's office, exchange pleasantries with the staff, and ask the Senate president if he had news or any other information he wanted to share. I would also proceed to the offices of the other senators—with Senator Guzman as my primary news source—and then to the speaker's office and the offices of the other members of the House of Representatives which was in the same building. My final stop was the office of the Washington representative, the islands' elected lobbyist in Washington, D.C. (The U.S. had not yet created a congressional seat for the island.) The governor and the Washington rep. usually eyed each other warily because what the rep.'s office might lack in terms of power it made up by the prestige attached to it. The rep. was the only other local official, besides the governor and the lt. governor, who was elected commonwealth-wide, and he usually wanted to be governor, too.

Once I said my hellos to the rep's staffers—he was usually in Washington, D.C.—I would exit the building and head to governor's office which was a few yards away to bother whatever officials, the governor hopefully, were there.

Covering Capital Hill involved a lot of photocopying, listening and tape-recording interviews. Legislative sessions, in particular, ate up a lot of one's time.

On that particular day, as I stepped into the Senate president's office, the door of his conference room was open, and I could see him with the other members of the majority, the speaker of the House, a middle-aged Japanese in a business suit, one of the governor's right-hand men, his special policy adviser (what exactly he did, not a lot of people knew), and *Tun* Jack. When he saw me looking at them, he smiled at me and nodded, stood up and closed the door.

Covering the political scene on a small island was teaching me a lot about how politics "worked." I had believed that political principles and/or ideologies guided or should guide politicians. And they did, more or less, particularly at the national level in certain democratic countries, but at the local level, politics was mostly who should get what, when, how—and who's paying for it.

I learned from one of the Senate president's staffers that the meeting was about a massive investment proposal from a group of Japanese businessmen. They were into hotels and travel agencies but now they wanted to upgrade the island's utilities and telecommunications system. The local government would soon announce a request for proposals or RFP.

I asked the Senate president after the meeting: "Sir, is it proper for government officials to meet in private with someone who is to submit a proposal for a government project?"

"*Lanya* Benj, there is no RFP yet," he said, "that was just a meet and greet."

The total cost of the projects was a cool $300 million.

"Please don't mention my name if you're going to write about our meeting," *Tun* Jack told me.

"Okay," I said.

"I'm just a friend of Sato san," referring to one of the Japanese businessmen.

I said nothing.

"By the way, I think I know now where to find the thing you want to see."

"The Amelia Earhart photos?"

He looked around. We were in the hallway outside the Senate president's office. "Walk with me to the parking lot."

50

T HE local economy was booming again. It hit some speed-bumps a few years back when Japan's economic bubble burst, but more Japanese and now South Korean tourists were visiting the island, and more businesses were opening their doors, including garment factories which had become the lightning rod for critics of local immigration and minimum wage control—including the influential U.S. garment lobby and their congressmen in Washington, D.C.

Garment factories on island, employing mostly foreign workers, were outcompeting the manufacturers on mainland America. The U.S. factories complained about the unfairness of it all. The unions said the factories were stealing jobs from U.S. workers.

The advocates of human rights were also unhappy. They said the conditions in the Saipan factories, which employed mostly skilled and experienced workers from China, were Third World-like. For appalled statesiders, the factories were "sweatshops."

Come to think of it, a lot of things appalled statesiders. Toilets that didn't flush. Cockfights. People who didn't speak English.

According to *The New York Times:*

"On this tiny, tropical outpost of the United States, many people describe what happens to foreign workers here as something close to servitude.

"Every year, thousands of laborers from China, the Philippines and elsewhere in Asia are flown here. The workers are often bused straight from the airport to squalid barracks where they live—sometimes for years—as many as a dozen to a room.

"They are put to work almost immediately in nearby factories within view of Saipan's pristine beaches, many of them laboring six days a week at about half the federal minimum wage, stitching together American brand-name clothes.

"The labels would be familiar to anyone who has strolled through an American shopping mall. Over the last year, Arrow, Liz Claiborne, The Gap, Montgomery Ward, Geoffrey Beene, Eddie Bauer and Levi's have all made clothes on this palm-fringed island that is part of the American commonwealth in the Western Pacific, 5,000 miles from the continental United States.

"And while many of these garments are manufactured in foreign-owned factories by foreign workers, the apparel made in the Northern Marianas often bears another familiar label: 'Made in the U.S.A.' The American flag flies over several of the factories.

"An estimated $279 million worth of wholesale clothing, virtually all of it made by foreign labor, was shipped from here last year to the United States.

" 'We come here because we make more money here than in China, and because the recruiters in China tell us that Saipan is part of America,' said a $2.15-an-hour factory worker from a village near Shanghai.

"The woman, who is in her early 20's, invited a visitor into the cramped barracks room that she shares with seven other women, their beds separated only by flimsy cloth sheets. The room also serves as a kitchen.

" 'They are not good conditions,' she says, wrinkling her nose and pointing to a mildewy hallway strewn with litter. 'If we complain, then our bosses would send us back to China and take away all of our money. Our families need the money.' "

The committee of the U.S. House of Representatives that had jurisdiction over the territories conducted an oversight hearing. Among those who testified was then-Governor Ramos, the predecessor of Governor Sanchez.

Ramos acknowledged that there were labor abuses, but added that those responsible had been charged and fined. He said there were other "isolated cases," and they would be dealt with in the proper manner. He said while these problems didn't originate with his administration— his predecessor was Sanchez's cousin—he would accept the blame for them.

Please remember, he said, "that we are new U.S. citizens. We are the newest members of the United States political family. New citizens always have some lessons to learn. New citizens sometimes make a mistake. We will make the necessary improvements…. Please have faith in the commonwealth you have created…. We are not a brutal people. We are not slave owners…. We, too, care about the human condition. Ours is basically a gentle, caring society. Today we have no homeless. We have no old folks homes. We have no hunger. Have a little patience with us."

The island's Washington representative, who would later unsuccessfully challenge the then-governor for their party's nomination, reminded the U.S. lawmakers about certain facts of life:

"Over the 30 years of the United Nations Trust Territory Administration [under the U.S.], we were taught that government employment held greater social prestige than business or manual labor. We were taught that discriminatory wage scales, based on race alone, were acceptable practice. This is the legacy we struggle to grow beyond…. I wish also to observe that our problems are not unique. [The committee chairman] helped uncover the presence of garment industry sweatshops in California, New York and Illinois 10 years ago…."

51

CCORDING to Manny, the "brouhaha"—his word—was the result of people looking at the same thing and not seeing the same thing. "It's about politics," he said, "mixed with economics and sprinkled with the gunpowder of race…"

"Race?" I asked.

"Statesiders. Islanders. Chinese. Filipinos."

"But…"

"And as usual, the statesiders will sound high and mighty, and the natives here will feel belittled and insulted, and some of the foreign workers will wonder out loud if the feds could give them green cards if the U.S. really believes the situation here is beyond the pale…"

"But it's not."

"It is for the statesiders. They can't deal with a less than perfect scenario…"

"But it's also happening in the U.S.!"

"And they will admit that, but they're in the saddle, not the island officials; the feds can change the rules here, and the local people can't do a damn thing."

"So what then?"

"Who knows."

"Will we get green cards if the feds take over immigration?"

"I don't know."

"Maybe, right?"

"The U.S. government is like a hippopotamus. It seems not to be moving, and is slow to react, but when it does, there's no escaping its immensity."

"Is that from *National Geographic*?"

"I borrowed a VCR tape from the library. Anyway, who knows what'll happen if the feds take over. If they do take over."

"But all this bad publicity…"

"You know in that last congressional oversight hearing, the richest haole on island…"

"Mr. Wood." He owned huge corporations doing business from the West Coast of the U.S. to the Philippines and all the islands in between.

"...he told the congressmen, that those who were complaining about the abuses here were statesiders, and that some of the allegations were just patently absurd—like the claim that all Filipina waitresses here were prostitutes..."

"Someone said that?"

"It was in the stateside-owned Guam newspaper— 3,200 Filipina prostitutes..."

"They had a headcount?"

"...the Philippine consul threatened a lawsuit..."

"Every Filipina waitress a prostitute!"

"Anyway, Mr. Wood had fun pointing out the exaggerations..."

"Well, this is not Saudi..."

"Or those other places where they slap their Filipina maids or rape them..."

The statesiders' frame of reference is life in the states, Manny added. "They think they know what life in the Third World is. They marry a Filipina and suddenly they're pretty sure how things are in the P.I., and they even have a pretty good idea how to fix the P.I. And so here, if a worker doesn't get paid for a month or more—it's slavery. In the P.I., it's called bad luck. The statesiders think we're 'docile.' They don't know we're as calculating as anyone else is on God's good Earth. We don't complain because we don't think it's to our advantage to do so. But we will once it is. Meantime, the statesiders want to save us from slavery and apartheid."

Sam says some of his fellow statesiders were kind of pissed that they were still kids in the 1960s and missed out on the civil rights movement. "They figured Saipan ought to do as the new battleground for civil rights with guest workers as stand-ins for 'Negroes.' " His two big, white hairy hands, doing air quotes.

"Your negroes were born and raised in the U.S.— were as American as the white people, but were deprived of their civil rights and their human dignity," Manny said, sounding like one of his editorials. "Foreign workers here are well, foreigners whose complaints are mostly of the breach-of-contract kind."

"We shall overcome," Sam said.

52

THREE months later, Sweet was back on island. When she wasn't around, I probably missed her. But while she was still in the P.I., Weng and I, now and then, would talk on the phone. And then for an entire week, her husband had to be on Rota and Tinian—he was performing a political chore, I suppose—so every night, for an hour or two, Weng and I would see each other. I would buy Miller Lite or wine coolers from the store where she worked, and we would drive to a beach, park my car, roll down the windows, sit back, drink and chat.

"Say it," I told her.

"What?"

"You miss me."

"Will you marry her when she gets here?"

"You really miss me."

"Of course you're going to marry her."

I said nothing.

"She's someone you can introduce to your mother."

I took a swig of my peach wine cooler. Yummy.

"Your mother knows her of course," Weng said.

"So how's married life," I asked.

"Changing the subject."

"Let's talk about you."

"Hmmph."

"And me. Missing each other."

She turned her head to her left and looked at me. "I wonder," she said before looking straight ahead again.

"What?" It was high tide. I could smell the Philippine Sea. Seaweed and dead fish. On the other side of the island was the Pacific Ocean and the abyss itself, the Marianas Trench.

"It was not meant to be," she said, but she sounded unconvinced.

"Who knows," I said.

"The old man is good to me."

I had nothing to say to that.

"And you're a good man so I don't think you'll break your girlfriend's heart."

"We should talk about happy things."

"When is she coming back?"

"Who?"

"You know who."

"Next week."

"What are we doing."

"Can I kiss you?"

"No."

We went out again a day before *Tun* Jack's return from Rota. It was Friday night so we could stay out late. "Doesn't he call you on the phone at night?" I asked Weng.

"He calls early in the evening. I told him I sleep at 8."

"No one checks you out at your house?"

"Sometimes his nieces drop by just to say hi. They're all nice to me."

"Do you love him?"

"I need him, I think. He wants me to get a green card. He says he trusts me."

"Are you crying? Don't cry."

"I'm just sad. Nothing happens like how it is supposed to happen."

"Are you sorry you met me?"

"Yes. No. I don't know."

That night we were drinking San Miguel Beer from the Philippines.

"I don't miss its taste," Weng said.

"But you miss me."

She sighed. I touched her hand. She didn't move it away. She looked at me, smiling now.

53

SWEET was paid way more than I was. "What do you expect?" Manny said. "She saves lives." And us? I asked. "We ruin them." We laughed. Sweet and I could have remained at our company barracks—my publisher didn't mind, but he said he would have to charge me for utilities at least, about $50 a month: power, water and sewer; not bad—but I wanted to have a place of our own. Just a small apartment with one room.

We found one in Chalan Kanoa, a 10-minute drive from the office, and near Sweet's clinic. We now could also afford to buy a car, and pay for it in monthly installments. We got married in the governor's office a week after she arrived on island. Otherwise, her parents would not have wanted her to move in with me.

During those days, Filipinos on island had to secure official documents from Manila to prove they were single. This became a requirement after it was learned that some very married Filipinos were marrying their new partners on island. Bigamy was—still is—a criminal offense in the P.I punishable by a six- to 12-year prison term. However, according to a Filipino lawyer who worked on island as a law clerk at a private law firm, bigamy committed outside the territory of the Philippines is not within the jurisdiction of Philippine authorities to prosecute. But if the bigamist returns to the Philippines with his second wife, and they live together as husband and wife, the first wife can file a criminal complaint for concubinage against the bigamist and his second wife.

Anyway, getting the official document from Manila involved a three-month waiting period, or so Manny told me.

"They'll also display your photos at the consulate in the meantime," he said.

"Like we're wanted criminals."

"Talk with Jim," the governor's spokesman.

I did, and Jim talked to the governor. The marriage licensing office was under the governor's office, and the person in charge was a local lady in her early 40s who was married to a younger Filipino dude still in the closet. Everyone on the island knew except, apparently, his wife. She was known to give Philippine nationals a hard time when applying for a marriage license. She was dead-set against older local men marrying younger Filipinas. But she was also *Tun* Jack's niece and, obviously, she had to give her beloved uncle a pass when he married Weng.

I was in the governor's office with the governor and Jim when he phoned *Tun* Jack's niece. They spoke in English and Chamorro.

"Just give him the license," the governor said, looking at me. "If he's already married in the P.I. then that's his problem." Jim chuckled. I smiled.

Sam and Manny, who also took the photos, were our witnesses on our wedding day. The ceremony was held in the governor's conference room. I wore a long-sleeved, lavender Ralph Lauren shirt and khaki pants. I was sweating as I stood there in front of the governor with Sweet who looked, as usual, fresh and refreshing. She wore a casual, knee-length, pink, sleeveless dress with a Peter Pan collar.

"*Lanya* Benj," the governor would later tell me. "She pretty, but why didn't you marry a U.S. citizen so I could have hired you already." We laughed.

Rob invited me and Sweet to visit him. He said Mila would cook *pancit* and broiled milkfish. We'd be drinking San Miguel beer, he said.

I was glad that he and Mila were together again.

"So where have you been?" I asked her in Rob's living room. Rob was in the restroom. We were having drinks—white wine—and watching TV; the Filipino channel.

"He's too much sometimes," Mila said, not looking at me. I wasn't that close to her, but I really wanted to know. "I thought," I said, "you had left him already."

"I did. But he begged me to come back."

"What happened?" It was Sweet's turn to ask. "He seems nice."

"Too nice," Mila replied. "To many other girls."

I chuckled. "Well, it's you he really wants."

"Who?" Rob said as he sat beside Mila.

"Nothing," she said. *Nahting.*

"So," Rob said looking at me, "what's up with Jack?"

"He's actually, really busy."

"I've heard he's in the thick of things."

"So it seems."

"It's going to be big."

"What do you know about it?"

"Something which can be nothing. But my main worry is the Amelia Earhart stuff he may or may not have."

"What do you mean?"

"He could be charged and jailed—"

"What?"

"—and someone else could get whatever the hell he says he has."

54

OB told me the story of a janitor who was arrested after telling Amelia Earhart's husband, the publisher George Palmer Putnam, that she was still alive. The janitor, Wilbur Rothar, demanded $2,000 for her safe return.

"When did this happen?" I asked.

"It was reported by *The New York Times* in Aug. 1937, about a month after her disappearance."

"How do you know?"

"My friend in the states, remember? I told you he has read all the relevant literature about this mystery."

"So what happened to the janitor?"

Rob said Rothar was from the Bronx, had a wife and eight kids. In 1934, at Roosevelt Field on Long Island, he was among the crowd of autograph-seekers who wanted to see Amelia Earhart make a routine landing in her plane. After she landed, "and as she was about to step from her plane, a wind blew her brown and white scarf" into Rothar's hands. He took it back with him to his Bronx apartment. Three years later, he showed it to Amelia's husband as "proof" that she was alive.

"What was his story?" I asked Rob.

He was supposedly a seaman on a vessel running arms to Spain where a civil war was still raging. He said the ship was on its way to Panama from New Guinea in the southern Pacific. "A few days out of New Guinea the skipper anchored off a small island to take on fresh water. In a cove on this island...a wrecked plane was discovered. The body of a man was lying on a wing of the plane. On the rocky shore a woman was standing in nothing but a pair of athletic shorts. The sharks...had eaten away the lower part of the man's body. The ship's crew buried the man at sea, and took the woman aboard. She was out of her mind, and badly injured."

"That Rothar dude sure could tell a story," I said.

"There's more. Lot's more," Rob said.

Rothar said a "Chinese doctor on board the vessel treated the woman for the rest of the voyage. It had been necessary...to give her blood transfusions. No one knew at the time who the woman was...but upon arriving in Panama they recognized her from newspaper photographs as Amelia Earhart. Members of the crew...became panic-stricken because they were afraid that their gun-running activity would be discovered if...Earhart were put to shore." The vessel proceeded to New York, and Rothar said the crew asked him to meet with Earhart's husband. Rothar told Putnam, "The boat has a lot of cutthroats aboard and they talked about dumping your wife into the sea." Rothar said Earhart was very ill and needed to be taken ashore soon to a hospital. But, he added, the crew wanted to be paid for rescuing her before they would turn her over. Putnam demanded that Rothar show him a lock of Amelia's hair or something to reassure him that they had her. Rothar said he'd bring something on the following day. What he brought was her brown and white scarf which Putnam did not recognize but his stenographer identified as one that Earhart had worn years ago. Putnam told Rothar to come the next day to get his money. Rothar showed up at Putnam's office and was given $1,000 cash and was on his way to a bank to get a check for an additional $1,000 when

Putnam's "secretary" who accompanied him arrested the scammer.

Rob said Amelia Earhart's sister, who wrote a biography of the aviatrix, told a different story regarding the same incident. An un-named ex-seaman, now a "young man," demanded $5,000 for disclosing the island in the Carolines where Amelia was held prisoner by smugglers. And the scarf was recognized by Putnam as belonging to his wife. But under "astute questioning," the fake informer was "caught in such a maze of contradictions" that he soon admitted that he was merely looking for easy money. Putnam didn't press charges, saying, "I know Amelia would not want it that way." He gave the ex-seaman $50 for the scarf and told him to "try going straight for Amelia's sake!"

Rothar, however, was indicted for extortion and was sent to a hospital in New York for "10 days of sanity tests." In Oct. 1937, he was committed to the Matteawan State Hospital for the criminal insane for treatment before his trial on the extortion charge. Rob said in 1966, Rothar's lawyer refused to answer any questions about his former client. In the same year, Rob added, almost 30 years after the event, the FBI special agent who appeared against Rothar in the commitment proceedings also declined to talk about the hapless extortionist.

And what happened to Rothar?

Rob said a thorough search of the New York City court records revealed that Rothar did not stand trial. Rothar also used the name Goodenough. Rob said there was no one named Rothar in any of the old or new New York phone books and city directories. And none of those named Goodenough said they were related to the man also known as Rothar. Moreover, according to the Matteawan State Hospital, Rothar was known as "Wilbur Rokar" and was transferred in 1960 to Harlem Valley State Hospital.

But "as with the name Rothar, no one named Rokar could be found listed anywhere in New York City."

"It's like a ghost story," I said.

Now according to Harlem Valley State Hospital, Wilbur Rokar was transferred to Central Islip State Hospital in March 1962.

And what did Central Islip say?

That Wilbur Rokar was discharged on Oct. 25, 1963 "at which time his whereabouts were unknown."

Records, however, showed that Rokar escaped from Central Islip State Hospital on Oct. 17, 1962 but returned on Oct. 29, 1963.

"Which kindda contradicted what the state hospital said about Rokar's release," Rob said.

"Kindda," I said. "Did anyone check the address of this Rothar/Rokar/Goodenough dude? The one mentioned by *The New York Times*?"

The address was 316 E. 155th Street.

Rob said: "There never has been a 316 E. 155th Street in NYC."

55

MARRIED life—mine, that is—was nothing to crow about. But I had no serious complaints either. I had known Sweet for, what?, five years before we got hitched. We got along for the most part, and we were still, I think, attracted to each other. We were young and approaching the prime of our lives, and we now had the opportunity to save money and make big plans for our future.

"You should get her pregnant," Noel said.

"We're trying," I replied. The act was becoming boring for me—a routine performed mindlessly like staring at the TV while flipping channels. Sweet was a nurse and she was monitoring her monthly ovulation cycle like Copernicus tracking the revolution of the heavenly spheres. She was also consulting regularly with the doctors and older nurses at the clinic where she worked.

We would get up at 6 in the morning. I would shower while she prepared our breakfast and her lunch which she would bring with her. I preferred eating in the office kitchen or driving back home where I would cook instant noodles and read whatever book I had with me. Her shift ended at 5. I could go home at 6, but Manny often wanted me to stay for an hour or more to help him put the paper to bed. He and Sam were grooming me for a bigger role in the newspaper, starting with writing editorials at least twice a week.

I'm usually at home at 8. My dinner was on the table and Sweet was watching TV. After eating, I would take off my shoes, socks, jeans and shirt, put on my house shirt, wash the dishes, brush my teeth and join my wife in our bed. I wore boxer shorts which I happily discovered on Saipan. I would only wear white briefs again if they were disposable and cost 10 cents each.

In bed, I would read a book or try to, but would usually end up watching Sweet's show, a Filipino variety show, sit-com, talk show or a tearjerker. Or we would chat for a while.

"How was your day."

"Okay. Yours."

"You know."

"Yeah."

"Yeah."

Friday evenings we would be at Rob's place or at a party or gathering of one of Sweet's co-workers. Every other Saturday, we would be at the Laundromat. Sweet also liked going to a different beach each week. One Friday evening, Sweet and I with Rob and Mila decided to hang out on a popular beach near a hotel, in the northern part of the island. We got there after dinner, at around 8. We had beer and wine coolers, chips and sandwiches, and Mila brought her boom box and a lot of extra batteries so we could play cassette tapes and dance on the sand. It was a full moon that night. Ron was shirtless and wore red pineapple print swim trunks. Like me, the girls wore t-shirts and shorts that weren't short. And they wore bras. There were other people on the beach, couples, too, but they were far from us.

So we swam (or, in my and Sweet's case, we walked into the surprisingly warm water), and then returned to the beach to drink and to talk about life in the P.I., the states and the island. Then we danced again, but I got tired quickly so Sweet and Mila danced with Rob who was enjoying himself as he goofed around with the two ladies while winking at me. Eventually, we were all seated on our beach towels, watching the enormous, red-orange moon that seemed to be setting on the horizon at dawn. We went home around 6 in the morning. I actually had fun.

On Sundays, I would leave after lunch and head to the office to file my stories. Sweet would watch TV all day.

Weng would usually give me a call after 6 whenever *Tun* Jack wasn't around. Weng seemed to be very interested in Sweet's maternal state.

"No," I would say. "She's not."

"Why not?"

"Well, what about you?"

"I don't think so."

"When can I see you?"

"What for?"

"I miss you."

An audible sigh.

"Drama queen."

"I'm hanging up."

"Don't!"

"Be nice then."

"I do miss you."

"Life goes on."

"Does it."

"You tell me."

I thought about Weng whenever I was with Sweet. No, I wasn't in love with more than one person. I wanted the one I couldn't have, and I was pretty sure I didn't want to lose the one who was already with me—but I also believed I could manage without her. I wanted Weng more. If we could be together, would I still want her?

"Maybe we should just run away together," I told her.

She laughed mirthlessly.

56

MANNY, my editor, asked me if I could imagine myself in another profession. Our publisher asked us the same question, months ago, but Manny said he wanted a serious answer this time. "I'm talking about another career," he said, "that can feed the family."

I wanted to be an architect after reading Ayn Rand's *The Fountainhead* when I was 16, but then my sister reminded me that I could not even draw stick figures if my ridiculous life depended on it, and that I loathed math. She was right. I was also too impatient and undisciplined to get a law degree. Since at least the fifth grade I wanted to be a writer. A playwright actually, like Shakespeare whose English I could barely understand until I was in college.

"I can't think of any other job for me," I told Manny. "Maybe a college instructor?"

"You need to get a master's degree and there are other requirements," he said.

"Oh. Well, then I'm sticking with this job."

"Maybe I could work in healthcare."

"Doctor? Nurse?"

"One of those dudes who look after old people. I'm talking about senior homes in the states. Or those kids with mental disabilities."

"Retarded?"

"I don't think you can call them that anymore. At least not in the states."

"You sound like you're seriously considering another profession."

Just thinking out loud."

Manny was already the longest serving journalist and editor on island. Local officials and other big shots knew him—and trusted his reporting skills. The statesiders grudgingly respected his work. "Well," one of them told me, "I don't agree with him all the time, and he can also be a jerk, but the man knows how to write in English."

"Respect the language," Manny would say. "The English language is our primary tool. But it is not ours. It is not the language of our soul. But that doesn't mean it can't be ours, too; that it can't speak to our soul. Respect the language. Never stop learning all about it. Cherish it. When you start dreaming in English, that means it has reached your very being." Manny, it turned out, was a philosophy major.

"Do you dream in English?" I asked him.

"Not yet."

Manny was a student at the state university which accepted only those who could pass its highly competitive entrance examination. And they were usually among the best and the brightest of P.I.'s high school graduates. He told me he never pictured himself as a writer although he liked reading, especially 19th century and early 20th century novels. He said Dostoevsky and Hemingway were his favorites. He said he was politically aware—he was in his teens during the heyday of the martial law regime—but not politically inclined. One of the term papers he turned in apparently made a deep impression on one of his professors who urged, if not ordered, him to apply for a spot on the news staff of the university's highly regarded, if not the P.I.'s most prestigious, student publication. Manny did and he was accepted. He was the publication's associate editor when he graduated from college. He then worked for what was then the P.I.'s top broadsheet. (There were three of them. All owned by our then-President-for-life Marcos and/or his cronies.)

He wanted to try something different, he said, when he accepted the job to edit a newspaper on Saipan. He ended up working for two of them, both owned by local politicians. The papers didn't last, but Manny had impressed the *Times'* publisher who offered him a job. Manny said he wanted to be back to his family in Manila. "I missed them—also, because I was leaving the island I finally received the four paychecks owed by my previous employer, so I was practically loaded. Yeah. The pay was good, but the paychecks were never released on time. There was a time when all I got on each payday was a $50 gift certificate so I could buy food and not starve to death. I couldn't get mad with my employer though. He was a good man but a not-so-good businessman." So Manny went back to the P.I. where he stayed for close to two years. Every time Sam was in Manila, however, he would call up Manny and try to hire him. "Eventually, I missed Saipan," Manny said. "So I came back."

Manny wasn't exactly popular among the *Times* staff. He was usually silent and unsmiling. But our newspaper's art and production departments knew that their work was easier because Manny was around. As a writer and editor, Manny was efficient and methodical. He could focus on the task at hand. He was also judicious. "When in doubt," he would tell his reporters, "don't." And: "If your mother says she loves you—verify." He was hard on himself and on everyone else apparently.

His wife on Saipan was pregnant with their second child, Manny told me.

"Congratulations!" I said.

"Yeah."

He also had two kids with the first wife in Manila. One was in 7th grade, the other was a 5th grader. His eldest on Saipan was 3 years old.

"I want my kids—my kids here—to grow up in the states which will be their world anyway when they grow up," Manny said. What he actually meant without saying it was that he wanted to go to the states and try to earn more money. But I would not realize that until much later.

57

MANNY was a contrarian. He said he had a deep-seated suspicion of, and/or distaste for, fads and all things "popular." One night at the office—we were the only ones left in the editorial room—he had a heated phone conversation with one of the leaders of the Filipino community on island. I never asked what it was about, but I clearly heard what Manny told his interlocutor.

"Brad," he said, using the Filipino slang for "brother," "Brad, I'm a reporter so I have no nationality. My passport says I'm Filipino, but when I write or edit the news I'm a reporter above all. I'm not supposed to lie or spread lies or enable lies. And I am not a cheerleader for our country or for our fellow Pinoys."

Manny was appalled when the Philippine government started calling overseas Filipino workers "new heroes."

"Jesus. So now all our heroes have to do is leave the country and remit money to their families back home. There was no need to risk their lives fighting our colonizers or invaders—it's all about sending money."

"Well," Noel said, "I don't give a crap what they call me. Just don't tax me and don't hassle me at the airport in Manila."

"And why do they say it's the Philippine government's policy to export labor?" Manny asked. "Were any of us ordered by our government to work abroad? It's up to us. We're in a democracy"—finger quotes—"and we've got the right to travel."

Never get Manny started with democracy.

"The ignorant and the uninterested choose who among the foxes should guard the hen house."

"So another dictatorship then?" I asked.

"No way. At least in a democracy, we can kick out the powers-that-be from time to time."

"But Lee Kuan Yew," Noel said.

"A rare breed," Manny replied. "So rare. One of the very few leaders who did not turn into a monster despite wielding so much power. But he governs a very small country whose people are mostly descendants of immigrants—hard-working, disciplined."

"And us?"

"We're the land of the fiestas, of showtime, of bombastic speeches and beauty pageants—where appearance is all."

"So we're doomed?" I asked.

"We'll be fine in our own way. I just don't expect us to become like Taiwan or Japan or South Korea. Which reminds me. Marcos admired the South Korean dictator Park Chung-hee. They're of the same age—"

"The dude shot by his intelligence chief?" I asked.

"Yeah. Marcos wanted to copy what Park was doing in South Korea. Like Park he picked businessmen who were supposed to create conglomerates like Samsung, Daewo, Hyundai with substantial help from the government. But most of Marcos's chosen cronies were incompetent capitalists."

"What do you think the problem is?"

"We're not Koreans."

58

SWEET and I were in the deepest stage of sleep very early one morning when a police officer knocked on our door. He and the other cops were going door to door to alert residents about a tsunami alert. We learned about it at just past 7, from a Filipino neighbor. He and his wife fled to the nearest higher ground at 5 a.m. and had just come back. It was a good thing that Sweet and I had slept through it all because I probably would have panicked, screamed and shrieked as I made a dash to our car. For Filipinos of my generation, a tsunami was the disaster that struck our southern island of Mindanao in Aug. 1976. Following an

8.0 earthquake, waves as high as 9 meters inundated communities along the shoreline. It was just after midnight, and most of the residents were sleeping. About 8,000 people died. Many bodies were never found.

Rob later assured me and Sweet that Saipan had never been hit by a tsunami in recent memory. By virtue of its location, he said, the island was apparently tsunami-proof. I hoped he was right. But a lot of people who lived near the shore, like us, freaked out that day. Especially the Chinese garment workers. Poor things. As if re-enacting Mao's Long March, hundreds of them left their barracks and walked all the way to Capital Hill even after the all-clear signal had been announced. Afterward, they almost caused a bank collapse as they withdrew their substantial savings and closed their accounts. Something clearly was missed in translation. Many of them were scared to death.

And then there were the typhoons. Filipinos are from typhoon country. I grew up hearing the names of howlers like Didang ("Dee-dung") and Sisang ("See-sung") which were uttered like curses. But experiencing typhoons on a small island in the middle of the Pacific, I soon found out, was different.

Like Manila, Saipan is in the tropics, but with more sunny days. When it rains, it seldom rains on the entire island—while driving, you will often see it's raining but three blocks away. When there is a tropical depression or a typhoon, however, the main concern on Saipan is the possibility of losing power. And no power means no water.

I would learn that the last time the island was directly hit by a typhoon was in April 1969. Her name was Jean and she destroyed 90 percent of the homes, and rendered another 8 percent unlivable. Food and water had to be airlifted from Japan, South Korea and Hawaii. But no lives were lost.

The other strong typhoon that caused major damage to the island happened 17 years later, in Dec. 1986.

Typhoon Kim's closest approach was 18 miles north of Saipan but a German lady who was residing on the island said it "was comparable to the bombardment she went through during the raids on WW II Frankfurt."

According to her husband: "First thing that happened was that the power went off—islandwide. Next thing, the telephones went dead.... We had built our office and home from concrete throughout, with typhoon exposure in mind. A good part of the local population, however, lived in simple wooden structures, several hundred of which were either blown away that night or washed out to sea. There was no more public water supply, and it took the authorities six weeks and longer to re-establish power and water. All trees on the island lost their leaves that night. What before was impenetrable rain forest was totally defoliated and suddenly looked like a ghostlike wilderness. Not to mention the broken-down power lines, flooding sewage, homeless, drowned boonie dogs, and the much higher than normal ocean level which now had submerged the protective reefs while heavy waves were still going strong. It was in that ocean where we cleaned ourselves up the next morning, soap in hand, and big fish swimming around...."

Happily, the typhoons that passed by the Micronesian region when I was on Saipan never came close to the island. But in the first year of our married life, Sweet and I had to endure two typhoons one after the other in a span of seven days.

"I hope it's not going to be like goddamn Kim again," Rob said. He wasn't on Saipan when Kim happened, but old-timers were only too eager to tell us about her whenever there was a typhoon advisory. Since Kim, moreover, most of the houses on island were already made of sturdier stuff—concrete. Sweet and I lived in one of them.

The first of the two typhoons approached the islands on Wednesday, and by early Thursday evening it was 110 miles east-northeast of Saipan. We were still trying to put the newspaper pages to bed. The newspaper office had a generator. The entire day was cloudy and rainy and then windy. In the afternoon, Manny, me and the other reporters were out on the road, taking photos. I could feel the wind from the sea buffeting my company car as I drove up Middle Road, north-bound before turning back to the office. Low-lying roads were flooded, but the water was only ankle-deep. Some roads were littered with stones and rocks from nearby hills, sharp enough to cause flat tires.

Sweet's clinic closed at noon, and she was already at home, calling me from time to time. Weng also called early in the evening, asking about the latest typhoon update. There was no longer power in their village, and she didn't have a transistor radio. Her husband was asleep. I asked if she needed anything, candles, etc. No, she said, they were OK. I miss you, I said. I miss you, she said, and then hung up. I went home sometime after 9. I was quite pleased with myself.

The following day, Friday, was still cloudy and windy, but there was no rain—and no power for the entire day which was humid, especially in the evening.

On Wednesday, the following week, we learned that another typhoon was making its way to the Micronesian region, and that it packed stronger winds than the previous one. It was also just 20 statute miles away as it passed over Saipan. This time, there were more flooded streets, more rocks and stones and tree branches littering the roads, and there was no power in our area for three days.

But again, Weng called me at the office, this time to tell me to be careful, and although I was cold and wet most of the day, and I could still hear the howling winds as I finally headed home in the evening, I was smiling.

59

CHRISTMAS in the Philippines starts on Dec. 1st and officially ends on Jan. 6th. It is festive and noisy. All the radio stations play Christmas songs. All the TV shows are flavored with Christmas themes. Christmas decorations are everywhere. And beginning on Dec. 16th, pre-dawn Masses that start at 4 a.m. are held in jam-packed churches. All throughout the Christmas season, groups of children or adults go house to house, singing carols until you either unleash the hounds on them (seldom happens) or give them a few of your inflated pesos. You can ignore them. But they'll keep on singing, off-key at that. So if you're neither deaf nor stone-hearted, you'll cough up the money.

On Christmas Eve, people who are not (yet) drunk go to church, but everyone has to be home before 12 midnight when we're supposed to eat a splendid Christmas spread whose centerpiece is usually a humongous ham and *Queso de Bola* or Edam cheese. Neither appealed to me. When I was a kid, presents were opened after dinner. Outside, the drunks got drunker and firecrackers got louder.

Christmas is a day- and night-long fiesta. All doors are open to everyone, and all homes serve food and drinks. Everyone is both a host and a guest. The neighbors drop by and you're expected to drop by at their homes, too. Children wear their new clothes and, for at least a day, they are rich beyond their wildest dreams. On Jesus's birthday in the P.I., the tradition is to give the kids money. For their part, grownups eat and drink a lot.

The culmination of the holiday season is New Year's Eve, Dec. 31st. The men start drinking at around 3 p.m. while roasting a pig—or a dog. Kids and teens start lighting up firecrackers in the streets. The louder, the better. In the evening, they will burn old tires in the middle of the street, and throw firecrackers at them. The womenfolk cook special dishes and place round fruits on the table—to attract prosperity in the new year. (Anything shaped like a circle will supposedly attract real coins—money.) All of us will be wearing red at midnight while filling our pockets with coins and jumping up and down like monkeys.

On the final New Year's Eve I celebrated in Manila before heading to Saipan, I joined a group of my old childhood friends—some had families already—in a drinking session that started just after lunch. Most of them smoked shabu—"ice" on Saipan, "crank," "crystal" or "meth" in the states. The problem with having ice heads as drinking buddies is that they can drink for hours without passing out. I staggered back to our house after 4, on the first day of the year. At 9 a.m., one of my drinking buddies was knocking on our door to tell me that they were still waiting for me to re-join them. They finally called it quits at around 8 in the evening.

Our city mayor implemented several programs to help combat shabu addiction, and it was a success, in a way. My ice-head buddies eagerly joined the mayor's anti-drug "sportsfest"—basketball, volleyball, chess, scrabble—and even won awards. Of course the mayor didn't know that the participating shabu users were also placing bets on each of the games. The loser had to buy the shabu. The winners would buy the beer. "Win-win!" as the P.I. president at that time would put it.

New Year's Eve in Manila, in any case, is like being in a war zone. So many fingers will be mangled by firecrackers; many shanties will burn down, and some will even die because of stray bullets fired by a drunk cop or soldier miles away, but each year it will be the same deafening celebration. Wherever you are at 12 midnight is ground zero. It is as if so many machine guns and artillery are being fired at the same time. Thick black smoke is everywhere. You'll wake up the next day with black boogers the size of bullets and just as hard.

So you can imagine how startling it was for me, and Sweet, to experience the holidays on Saipan for the first time. It was…serene. Not a lot of noise or even firecrackers on New Year's Eve. People on the island preferred a dazzling fireworks display. And the holidays weren't as raucously decadent as they were in Manila.

"You'll get used it," Manny said. "I actually like the way it's celebrated here. Low-key. Solemn moments befitting the occasion are not drowned out by noise, so there's more of those moments here, and they're easier to recognize and appreciate."

"You're getting soft chief," I said.

60

H

ELL, Manny said, was about to break loose. The cabinet secretary responsible for multi-million-dollar infrastructure projects had just been caught *in flagrante delicto* with his young secretary in his office by his wife. We learned that it wasn't the first time that the cabinet secretary had been fooling around, but now his wife had had enough and was no longer taking it, well, lying down. She went to the legal counsel of one of the companies that had submitted a proposal for the projects. She told him that her beloved husband and other administration officials had been secretly meeting with another company in Japan, all expenses paid by said company, to discuss how they could "fix" the request for proposals so that the contract could be awarded to said company. She signed an affidavit and enlisted the support of one of the island's more blatantly self-serving yet cunning senators, the governor's pet peeve, Orlando Jimenez, who vowed to tell all and name names.

At that point, no one in the media had seen the contents of the affidavit, but Jimenez hinted that Mrs. Cabinet Official had a lot of details backed with documentation, including receipts and even photos. Apparently, her husband and the company executives had been meeting quite a lot, usually in Tokyo or in Manila.

Manny said no one else in the Senate wanted to cast his lot with Mrs. Cabinet Official—yet. But Senator Jimenez, who at that point was the one-man minority bloc, had nothing to lose. He wasn't up for re-election. And perhaps he was thinking that the administration would find ways to calm him down, so to speak, in a manner that was mutually beneficial.

"I can't stand whores in politics," Manny said. "And most of them are. Including voters."

Everyone on island was talking about the scandal that had not been reported yet by the media because no one wanted to talk about it on or off the record. U.S. federal money was involved which meant a possible exhaustive and exhausting federal investigation that would be followed by a grand jury, indictments, trial, sentencing, prison in the states.

"That's why smarter politicians don't mess with federal money," Manny said, referring to the island officials who had ended up in the federal slammer for corruption charges.

"But no federal money has been spent yet," I said. "Right?"

"I guess. But can this administration survive such a scandal?"

"What do you think?"

"What would voters think once we put it on the front page?"

"If we get a copy of the affidavit."

"Jimenez won't give to us. Unless…"

"What?"

"The governor refuses to bargain with him."

"It goes all the way to the governor?"

"I don't think anyone in the executive branch can fart without the governor's permission."

I no longer remember how, or if he ever told who his source was, but Manny managed to get a copy of the affidavit which, by then, had been attached to a complaint filed under seal in court by one of the not-so-well-connected companies competing for the contract.

Manny had covered all the beats on island, and his "secret" in getting the information he wanted or needed was based on his realization that to have access to government officials, you had to go through their secretaries and/or staffers. Manny knew them all, and called them by their first names. He also knew their and their children's birthdays and wedding anniversaries. He would print "happy birthday" or "happy anniversary" greetings in the paper with their photos. He would talk to them about their kids. He never said anything bad about anyone and never broke his promise to keep certain things "off the record." He also gave them complimentary copies of the *Times*.

If Manny didn't know you, he would strike you as someone indifferent, aloof. If he knew you, however, he could turn on the charm or what might as well pass for it.

And so, *voila*. Someone, somehow had handed him a copy of a document that no one else, especially the press, was supposed to see. But because the case had been sealed, we still could not quote from the affidavit or write a news story about it.

"Talk to the governor," Manny told me.

"You mean Jim," I said referring to the governor's spokesman.

"Yeah. Scare him shitless."

He meant that I should ask questions indicating that we knew more than we're letting on.

Jim, however, turned out to know nothing about it.

"Swear to God, I'm not in the loop," he told me over the phone. He was on speaker phone. Manny was listening. "You can't quote me on anything," Jim added.

"Way off-the-record, this conversation," I said.

"You're fishing and—"

Manny cut in. "Jim, we know already."

"Manny? I don't know what you're talking about."

"We know the allegations—all the details."

"The governor is not involved."

"How do you know? You just said you don't know anything."

"Manny, you know what I mean. We consider you a friend."

"Well, then, as a friend please pass along what we've just discussed to the governor."

Manny expected a call from the governor. We did receive a call. I did. But not from the governor.

"*Lanya* Benj." It was *Tun* Jack.

61

MANY years later, I would read a book about the most notorious lobbyist in U.S. history, one of whose clients was the island government. He supposedly said, "The worst thing you can do is to approach someone the first time you meet them and ask for help. That's not how human nature works."

Old man Jack knew human nature.

"Long time!" he said over the phone. Long time no see. "I'm having barbecue at the beach this Saturday with the wife and some friends. Come on over. Let's talk about Earhart. Bring your wife and your haole friend and his girlfriend."

"Friday, so tomorrow?"

"Just before lunch. I have this special spot at Kilili Beach. My nephew will sleep there tonight to make sure it's reserved for us." The old man laughed. He sounded like a salesman laughing at the joke of a potential customer.

I told Manny about it. "Hear him out," he said.

We arrived at the beach just before noon. The sun was out, the sky was clear. The lagoon sparkled. Just another day in paradise.

A young local man, one of *Tun* Jack's nephews, was grilling baby back ribs. On a long wooden table were sinful trays of Chamorro rice, green salad, fried chicken, pickled cucumbers, grilled hotdogs, sashimi. There were ice-cold Budweisers and Miller Lites in coolers as well as soda and bottled water.

Tun Jack was seated with a group of men at another wooden table while Weng and three middle-age ladies were playing cards at a white picnic table. He stood up and shook my and Rob's hands and said hi, shyly, to Sweet and Mila. Weng invited them to sit with her and join the game. "We're playing for quarters only," she said smiling ever so kindly. She looked so attractive in her pink shorts and white V-neck, sleeveless blouse. Could the old man get her pregnant? But I couldn't look at her for too long. Her husband was introducing me and Ron to his friends, elderly local men. They, too, had heard about Amelia Earhart on Saipan.

It was a pleasant gathering. The girls played cards, laughed and talked and laughed some more. At our table, no one talked about religion or politics, just pleasantries until the conversation inevitably drifted to Earhart. One of

Tun Jack's friends, another retiree, recounted a visit in December 1960 of two haoles in search of Amelia. The statesiders talked to a local man who said he saw a plane crash on a beach and there were two people in it—an American man and woman, and both were imprisoned by the Japanese. The visitors also talked to another local man who lived on the main floor of a hotel where Amelia and her navigator, Fred Noonan, were supposed to have been interned for a week before they were taken away by the Japanese. When shown a photo of Earhart, the local man said she looked like the American girl at the hotel, but he couldn't be sure about it. But when shown Noonan's photo, he said: "This is the man who stayed at the hotel."

The statesiders also talked with a local woman who worked as a servant in the hotel. She said she saw two Americans in the back of a three-wheeled vehicle—their hands were bound behind them, and they were blindfolded. One of them was a woman. When shown a photo of Earhart and Noonan, the local woman said, "They look like the same people I saw, and they are dressed the same way." So what happened to them? "I only saw them once in a three-wheeled truck. I don't know what happened to them."

Another local man told the visitors from the U.S. that he saw a "white man and woman" at the Japanese military headquarters on island. They were supposedly flyers and spies. Another local woman who, as a young girl, lived with her family next door to the Japanese hotel before the war, said she saw an American girl in the hotel. The American visited her and her sister at their home. What did she look like? "She was dressed in a cloth trench coat. The first time I saw her she looked very pale as though she were sick. She wore no make-up. My sister and I offered her food. She accepted it but ate very little, only a little fruit." When the American visited them again, "she had bandages on her left forearm—also bruises or burns on the right side of her neck." The American girl liked the local woman's sister "very much, and on this second visit when my sister was doing a geography lesson, the American girl helped her draw correctly the location of the Mariana Islands in relation to other islands in the Pacific."

The American girl stayed at the hotel for seven days, the local woman said. "A bus boy who worked at the hotel told me the America girl died there. He said the bed she slept on was soaked with blood and that before she died, the American girl had been going very often to the outside toilet." But the local woman didn't know where the American girl was buried. When shown several photographs of Amelia Earhart, the local woman said, "It looks like the same girl."

62

BEFORE we left the beach just after the sun set, *Tun* Jack told me he wanted to see me again, "somewhere more private," he said. He told me to visit him at his house. This is it, I thought. He'll try to talk me out of writing about the looming scandal involving the administration. But when we met again at his house, he still went on and on about Amelia Earhart—it was as if he was merely resuming our conversation on the beach.

The old man's house was a modest-looking, cream and red bungalow with an open garage where his dark-blue Nissan Pathfinder was parked. The house had several bedrooms and a spacious living room with a brown soft leather sofa set, a bare coffee table and floor lamps. On the wall was a Persian tapestry with a peacock-tail design.

"Weng is my interior decorator," *Tun* Jack said as if it explained everything. I wanted to ask where she was, but I couldn't. "She's in the room," her husband said as if reading my mind, "watching TV."

We sat down facing each other at the brand-new-looking dining table with four chairs. He then stood up and grabbed a couple of Miller Lite beers from his expensive looking refrigerator and opened a can of Planters cocktail peanuts.

"You already had dinner?" he asked me. It was a weekday. I just came from work.

"Yes," I lied.

"Because I can ask Weng to cook soba," the old man said. Soba on the island usually referred to instant noodle soup with Tinian pepper, crushed ginger, slices of hard-boiled egg and Spam.

"No I'm fine sir," I said, munching on peanuts before sipping my beer.

"I think I now know where to find what you gentlemen want me to find," he said smiling before drinking his beer.

"Dad." It was Weng walking toward the refrigerator. She was in a white nightgown, sleeveless and above-knee length. Breathtaking.

"Hi *kuya*," she said to me without looking at me as she took out a can of Diet Coke from the fridge and walked back to their bedroom.

Her husband was looking at me, still smiling.

"So you were saying," I said.

"They're not bones after all," he replied. "But photos and some clothing. One of the haoles who were here in 1960 came back the following year and dug up some bones which he shipped to the U.S. They were supposed to belong to Earhart and her navigator. But an anthropologist in California said the bones belonged to Chamorros." He chuckled.

"So when can we see those photos?" I asked.

"I've already told my nephews to help me look for the box where the photos are."

"Where is the box?"

"It's either in the house of a relative here on Saipan or on Tinian."

I chuckled.

"I'm not pulling your leg Benj. The box exists, the photos and clothing exist. And I will give them to you."

"Okay."

"I need to give them to you."

Here it comes, I thought.

"I help you and of course you help me, right?"

I smiled.

"We're friends Benj," the old man said.

I

had to ask Rob to explain to me what he believed happened to Earhart and Noonan—who was trying to cover up what and why. First of all, he said, there was no mystery about it. "Their plane crash-landed somewhere in the Marshall Islands area, and they were picked up by the Japanese and later flown to Saipan, which was then Japan's military headquarters in the Northern Marianas. They were considered spies and they eventually died at the hands of their captors. They were probably buried on Saipan—or on Tinian."

Were Earhart and Noonan spies?

"They were on a mission on behalf of the U.S. government which wanted to know the exact locations of Japanese military installations in Micronesia."

"But then their plane crashed?"

"That was part of the plan man. They were supposed to get 'lost' for a while so the U.S. Navy could rescue them."

"But—

"The Japanese got 'em first."

"Why didn't they announce it to world?"

"She was the most famous woman in the world man, and she was looking for evidence of Japanese military fortifications that were supposed to be top secret because they were illegal. Also, the Japanese navy wanted to keep her plane, take it apart, check out its technology."

"Why didn't the U.S. raise hell?"

"And admit that we were spying on the 'Japs'?" Air quotes with his fingers. Rob was PC. "They did a movie about it!" he added. "In 1943!"

Flight to Freedom starred Rosalind Russell as Tonie Carter, the world famous aviatrix, and Fred MacMurray, as her navigator and love interest Randy Britton. After Tonie announced that she would circumnavigate the globe on a solo flight, she was approached by a U.S. admiral who asked her to go on a top-secret mission. It involved flying over the Japanese mandated islands in Micronesia. The mission, the admiral told Tonie, was "one of the most vital in the history of our country," and she was "the only person in the world who can do it." The mission "will require a year, perhaps two, perhaps three. And it will be highly dangerous. It will be necessary for you to give up, temporarily, we hope, everything you love, because the world has got to think you are dead. Upon the success of this—and believe me, I am not exaggerating—may depend the fate of the United States of America." But "if there is any slip-up at all, you yourself will have to suffer the consequences. This country cannot intervene. The possibility of death is very great."

Of course Tonie Carter volunteered for the job.

"You will fly around the world again," the admiral told her, "but this time you will reverse your direction.... This will give the world time to get really interested in your flight. But here, somewhere in this area you will get into trouble. You will radio an SOS—you will make it sound as hopeless as possible. But you will be sure the world hears it. That will give us a chance to do our job."

Tonie was supposed to land on "Gull Island" which "is less than two miles square and only twenty feet above sea level." It would be provisioned and stocked. She was instructed to remain there "until the Navy comes and takes you off." According to the admiral, "that may be a week, a year…but at any rate, it will enable us to serve our purpose. That is, a great and widespread search for you somewhere in the ocean. Only we shall look for you with photographic planes." The admiral said only Tonie's "predicament" could justify such a search by air over what the U.S. believed were fortified Japanese islands. "There is an emotional difference," the admiral said, "between a man falling in the ocean and a woman. Especially Tonie Carter."

However, in Lae, New Guinea, the last stop before Tonie and her navigator set out for Gull Island, a Japanese hotelkeeper told her: "Imperial Japanese Navy reports that many provisions have been left at Gull Island for you. It may interest you to know that the Japanese government is fully aware of what you are doing and that you will pretend to disappear in the sea. Within ten minutes after your disaster is announced, a Japanese plane will be notified and it will be quite unnecessary for the United States Navy to send planes to look for you over Japanese mandated islands. Thank you, please."

Undeterred, Tonie deliberately crashed into the sea so that she could truly be lost which allowed U.S. planes from Navy ships to search for her over the fortified Japanese mandated islands with cameras.

"OK," I said, "assuming that the movie got it right, why is it still a secret 50 years after the war?"

"Japan doesn't want to admit that it had captured Earhart and Noonan and that they died in Japanese custody. The U.S. has no interest in dredging up an inconvenient historical fact involving what is now its most important ally in Asia."

Rob's friend, Fred, had a more complex theory: Earhart was brought to Japan where she was interned. Japan copied her plane's technology in creating the Zero which proved lethal in the early years of the war in the Pacific. These details, if disclosed, were just too embarrassing for the U.S. which preferred the more widely accepted story that Earhart and Noonan had died somewhere in the Pacific when their plane crash-landed. In exchange for not charging the Japanese emperor with war crimes, Japan agreed to keep Earhart's capture a secret. Shortly after the war, she returned to the U.S. with a new identity.

"Why," I asked Rob, "do some people choose to believe grandiose explanations?"

"There were so many witnesses man! Islanders and statesiders!"

"There's always the grassy knoll," I said.

"I watched that movie," he replied, referring to Oliver Stone's *JFK,* "and it's probably what really happened in Dallas anyway."

"But what if the simplest, most boring theory is actually the truth?"

"You're sticking to the 'official' story huh," he said grinning as he looked at me like I was his favorite red-neck cousin.

"Earhart and Noonan ran out of fuel and crashed in the Pacific," I said.

"There was a cover-up and a conspiracy!"

"Do you believe man really landed on the moon?"

"Har-har. Didn't your old friend say he has proof? Don't believe me then. Believe what your eyes tell you!"

"What will I see?"

"When will he show it to you anyway?"

T*UN* Jack and I met again, this time at the governor's office. It was a Friday afternoon and I was just stepping into the lobby when I saw him going down the stairs and behind him was the governor himself. "There he is," the big man said, smiling at me. "What's the scoop today Mr. Benjie?" "You tell me gov," I replied. He then spoke in Chamorro with *Tun* Jack who nodded and said, "*hunggan*." Yes. "Well, I gotta run," the governor said. "Meeting," he added as he walked out of the building before I could say anything further.

"I think I have it," *Tun* Jack said.

"It's with you right now?" I asked.

"No *lai*," he said. "Walk with me to the parking lot." So I did. "My nephew," he said, "found the box, I think."

"You think?"

"I'm not stalling, Benj. I know what I have, and I have it."

"That's what you keep telling me."

"And I will show it to you."

"Now?"

"Now."

"Really?"

The old man nodded.

"The governor himself told me to give it to you."

"I understand." I did.

"I'm glad."

"So where is it?"

"It's in my house. Follow me."

It was a 10-minute ride from Capital Hill to his place. Weng wasn't around, but her presence was everywhere in the house. I even imagined that I could smell her cologne as I sat on their sofa.

"Coke? Water?"

"Water please, thank you." I was thirsty and was genuinely grateful for the long tall glass of cold water that the old man handed me with a stylish wood coaster. I was not in hurry. I was also hoping that Weng would arrive soon.

Her husband sat facing me across the coffee table.

"I like what my wife has done to this house," he said, looking around him.

"Can't argue with that," I said.

"When will you invite us to your place?"

"It's a small one-room apartment," I said, smiling. "I don't think more than two people could fit in there."

"I bet it's cozy."

"It is."

He pointed to a box I hadn't noticed on the floor beside the sofa where I was seated. It was a white storage box which I had previously seen only in American movies. You know, that scene at the office after the hero is told to clear out his desk when he is putting all his stuff in the box. *That* box.

"Can I take a look?" And I pointed at the box.

"You know," the old man replied, "the governor is really trying his best."

Okay, I thought, but I didn't say anything.

"He is trying to change the old ways of doing things, you know. It's hard."

I nodded.

"He wants what's best for the local people and also for our guest workers. He's a friend to Filipinos."

"I think he's doing great," I said while casting a glance at the box.

"But not everyone's happy with what he's doing."

"That's how it is I guess."

"They're spreading rumors about him—lies."

"Well..."

"Are you going to write about it?"

Did he know what we knew? I said: "Are we talking about—"

"He's not involved in it."

"So—

"But they will insist he is, and they will lie and lie…"

"I—"

"So you have to be fair Benj."

"I am. We are."

"That lady's affidavit—"

"We will—"

"…lies, and her husband—he's a nephew—but he's also an idiot, and that's not the governor's fault."

"I don't—"

"It will be election season soon, and all we ask is fairness from you guys."

"Sure."

"We don't care about the other newspapers, no one believes them."

I chuckled.

"You want more water?"

"Yes please." I was still thirsty.

He refilled my glass.

"You want to have dinner here? You go pick up your mrs. and come back later. Weng will be here early. I'll ask her to get food from this Japanese restaurant."

It was tempting. I really wanted to see Weng. But.

"It's OK sir," I said, "I still have work to do and the mrs. may have OT tonight."

"She should work at the hospital," *Tun* Jack said, smiling. He meant she could be paid more.

"Oh," I said.

"The governor can make it happen, you know."

I smiled.

"And anyway your mrs. for sure is an experienced and qualified nurse. What our hospital needs."

I told him Sweet did apply at the hospital, but she was told there was no vacancy.

"I think she should apply again," the old man said.

"OK," I said, pointing again at the box.

"Take it *lai*—we appreciate your friendship."

Not the royal "we." He meant him and the governor.

"Call me," *Tun* Jack said, "if you need anything else."

65

I DROVE to the office and showed my publisher and editor the box which I placed on the coffee table in Sam's room. The three of us—he, Manny and I—stood around it as if we're staring at a newly unearthed buried treasure...or a ticking bomb that we didn't know how to disarm.

"Did you take a peek," Manny asked me.

"No," I said. "But..."

"What," Sam said.

"I think they want something for it in return," I said.

"*They*?" Manny asked.

"The governor," I said.

"The governor, of course," Sam said.

"And I think I kinda said that we can return the favor."

"Kinda?" Manny said.

"Which means," Sam said, "he believes that you—*we*—will give them what they want."

"There's another thing," I said.

"What," Sam said.

"I think they'll give my wife a job at the government hospital."

Manny chuckled.

Sam looked at me. "I didn't need to know that, but I appreciate your honesty."

Manny chuckled again.

"They got us," Sam said. He and Manny looked at each other.

"What?" I asked.

"Should we honor it?" Manny asked Sam.

"What?" I asked.

"They could give us hell," Manny replied.

"What?" I asked. Then I finally understood. "I didn't promise anything."

"You didn't have to," Sam said.

"You took the box," Manny said.

"You take, you give," Sam said.

"Should I return the box?" I asked.

"Don't be silly," Sam said.

"There are other ways to get the other story," Manny said, referring to the corruption allegations.

"How?" I asked.

"Senator Jimenez," Manny said.

"You're assuming he'll sing," Sam said.

"Yeah. But he's always for sale," Manny said.

"Hah," Sam said.

"The wife," I said, referring to the mrs. of the hapless cabinet secretary, Chuck Tolentino.

"She's with Jimenez," Sam said.

"She's hoping Jimenez will go after her husband and his boss, the governor," I said. "Right?"

"What if she wants to gets something else from the governor?" Manny said.

"Like what?" I asked.

"It could be anything," Sam said.

"Like the governor publicly firing her hubbie," Manny said.

"A government job for her somewhere else: on Guam or in the states." Sam said. "Maybe a business loan."

We were still looking at *Tun* Jack's box.

Sam opened it and took out several old photos and documents in a clear plastic container and a very old looking man's shirt, which probably was originally white, with short sleeves and an open collar.

Sam placed the box on the floor and spread the photos on the coffee table. There were 11 of them of various sizes, the largest of which was about 5 x 8 inches. They were black and white. Actually gray and white and yellow. Some were cracked, and others were hopelessly faded. They were photos apparently taken on Saipan, during the Japanese administration in the 1930s.

"This should be Garapan back then," Sam said, looking at one of the photos.

"Everyone's Japanese," Manny said staring at the photos.

"Hello," Sam said. He showed us a photo of what appeared to be a Caucasian man and woman posing with several Japanese military officers. Most of the faces were faded or fading."

"That may be her," Manny said, referring to what appeared to be a woman in one of the photos.

"Well I'll be," Sam said.

She was wearing dark pants and a white shirt with short sleeves and an open collar.

"Are we seeing what we think we're seeing," Sam asked, "or are we seeing what we want to see?"

66

I T'S raining, Manny said, and pouring. I had just "stumbled onto" a sworn document, an affidavit from one of the governor's Japanese business friends—one of his oldest campaign donors, Taka *san*—who was involved in an ongoing civil lawsuit after a falling out with a former business partner. Taka *san* was deposed by the opposing counsel, and what he revealed under oath could be fatal to the governor's political career.

"How did you get this?" Manny asked me while reading the court document.

"You know," I said. It was lunch break and I just came from Capital Hill. Manny and I were the only people in the editorial room.

"Jimenez." Manny said.

"One of his community workers." I literally bumped into him as he was leaving his boss's office.

According to the sworn statement, Taka *san* admitted that a year or so ago, he arranged a meeting between the governor and other Japanese investors interested in doing business on Saipan. They all agreed to raise a total of one-hundred-thousand dollars for Taka *san* who could then "lend" the money to their politician friends in the CNMI—i.e., the governor.

"A slush fund?" I asked.

"By any other name."

"But Taka *san* says it's a loan."

"Sure. We showed the affidavit to Sam. "My God," he said. "He's going to be beaten black and blue," referring to the governor.

"Jimenez's staffer told me they gave it only to me," I said.

"As wily as ever," Sam said.

"Hmm," Manny said.

"What?" I said.

"He gives it to us only so if we don't run it..." Manny said.

"He'll know we've been 'bought,' " Sam said with air quotes.

"We can do the story," I said. "But we won't run the, uh, other one," I added referring to the affidavit of the cabinet member's wife.

"OK," Sam said. "We'll find out how we can do that without reneging on the promise that they thought we made to them when we accepted the box."

"But we've to get a comment from the governor's office," Manny said.

"Taka's affidavit?" I asked.

"We have to get the governor's side," Sam said.

So I called the governor's office and asked Jim for comment.

"I've got to see that affidavit first," he said.

So I faxed it. Then I called again.

"Yeah," Jim said, "shit, excuse me. I'll call you back."

It was Sam who received a phone call, from the governor no less. Manny and I were in his office at the time.

"To what do I owe this honor governor?" Sam said. "OK, uh, Ed." He chuckled. "OK. All right. Sure, sure. Tomorrow then."

The governor had invited him to lunch at a golf course.

Later, I also received a phone.

"My friend." It was *Tun* Jack.

67

MANNY said he was sick and tired of being used by politicians. "Well," he added, "we use them, too, but still." We were in the newsroom. He had just put all the pages to bed. I was late in filing my stories—I had to cover back-to-back legislative sessions—and when I was done, Manny asked me to proofread the foreign news and business sections. He wanted me around so he could vent when the rest of news staff had left. The other reporters, he once told me, considered their jobs as jobs: something to do to get paid.

"But you," he said, "seem to think what we do is important."

"It's not?" I replied.

"Don't tell anyone."

But that's just Manny. I now think he liked to sound aloof and cynical so no one would know how dead serious he was—how deeply he cared for his profession, and what he believed it meant to civilized life.

"These officials like to mess things up, and we're supposed to cover it up or deodorize it," he said.

Since I landed on Saipan, I had been hearing a lot about him from my reporter friends in Manila through snail mail which was the only kind of mail back then. I sent them Christmas cards the first year of my life on island, and we ended up pen-pals for a while. I asked about the latest news—i.e., gossip about our other friends—back home while they asked me about how my life was on Saipan. When I mentioned that Manny was my editor, they told me they had heard quite a lot about him when he was still in Manila. Photographers didn't like him—because he would tell them to refuse the cash doled out by staffers of government officials. Some editors didn't like him much either. They, too, were on the take, and they didn't want him mucking up what many considered a time-tested arrangement between the Fourth Estate and the powers-that-be.

Complaining about corruption in the P.I., Manny once told me, is like complaining about the heat in the Sahara Desert. "Corruption is not a problem back home," he said. "It is a permanent condition—things as they were, as they are, and will ever be."

"We need a revolution," I said, hoping it wasn't true.

"Yeah. Kill all the adults. Let the kids take over."

"Pol Pot?"

"*Lord of the Flies.*"

I chuckled.

"No," he added. "Our culture must change. But it seems that culture is like DNA."

"Destiny."

"I refuse that destiny."

"You and who else?"

"Hah."

"No," I said. "We'll come around one of these days."

"Look at how it is on this tiny island, just because the American flag flies here. Sure, there's corruption but if you get caught, especially by the feds, then *sayonara.*"

"How can we have that respect for the law?"

"That is the question. Marcos already tried tough love."

"He was the primary lawbreaker."

"Power corrupts. Yet we all believe it'll be different somehow if the right leader comes along."

"We need the right leaders?"

"We need the right voters. So we're doomed, I tell you, doomed."

Manny said he didn't want to play ball with politicians anymore—in the P.I. or on Saipan.

"I'll tell Sam we have to run the story about the affidavit from the cabinet secretary's wife and the affidavit of the governor's Japanese friend.

"What about the Amelia Earhart stuff?" I asked.

"It's ours already. We'll also break the news."

"So *pak* 'em all basically."

"*Pak* 'em all."

"And then?"

"The *pak* if I know."

68

S AM said he and the governor played golf and had lunch. The governor was alone, but Sam said as he was leaving the hotel, he saw *Tun* Jack in the lobby. "So what did he say boss?" Manny asked Sam. We were in Sam's room. The Amelia Earhart box was still on the coffee table. Sam was at his executive desk while Manny and I were seated in the desk chairs.

"We talked about golf," Sam said. "Then we talked about the good 'ol days. Then Amelia Earhart. Then..."

Manny and I looked at him.

"He talked about his plans. They sound great. Forward looking. He hit the right notes, for my benefit of course. He also told me that he wants my wife, who is somehow related to him, he said, to serve on a government board—any board; whichever she wants. And he said he will have to rely on my advice from now on."

"Of course," Manny said.

"Yeah," Sam said. "Of course." He added, "The most important task now, he told me, is to sustain the momentum for reform, under his administration, and prevent sonsofbitches like Jimenez from derailing it. He believes Jimenez will run against him. 'I'm not a saint,' the governor told me. 'But that guy's the devil.' "

"So in short." Manny sounded impatient. Sam looked at him as if he were looking at an impertinent favorite child.

"In short," Sam said, "he'll continue to fight corruption, but the problem is, he's the one who is now being accused of what he wants to 'eradicate.' His words."

"You believe him?" Manny asked Sam.

"He said he's signing an open government bill once it lands on his desk. He's firing Tolentino and canceling the procurement for the projects. And he says he's paying his debt to the Jap, uh, nese."

"All in a day's work," I said.

"And we also have the Earhart exclusive," Sam said.

"That'll land us on the front pages of U.S. newspapers—the TV networks!" I said.

"Truth, justice and the American way." Sam seemed to be teasing Manny who looked unimpressed.

"We should still run the stories about the affidavit and the deposition, but with comments from the administration."

Sam said nothing.

"Jimenez called me earlier," Manny said. "He's willing to go on record."

"Whoa," I said.

"Really," Sam said.

"Really," Manny said.

Sam said nothing.

Manny said: "Did you promise—"

"No Manny, I didn't promise anyone anything." Sam sounded peeved.

"Jimenez wants you to interview him tomorrow morning in his office," Manny told me. "If it's OK with the boss," he added.

"Do what you've got to do," Sam said and he stood up, ending our meeting.

69

I'VE a lot of bombs to explode," Senator Jimenez told me. We were in his office, the one next to the men's restroom in the Senate portion of the legislative building. "That's what you call it, right, *bomba*," he added, smiling as he gestured with his hands as if they had just detonated.

"That was in the early 70's sir," I said. I wanted to add, "I was still a toddler," but I didn't want to sound rude. He seemed like someone who could literally throw me out of his office.

"Yes, Marcos was still your president," Jimenez said. "Brilliant man."

I didn't say anything.

"Maybe too brilliant for his own good."

Like the governor, Senator Jimenez was in his early 50's. He was tall, but not as tall as the governor, and of medium build. His hair was dyed black and pomaded and he wore clear glasses that made him look like a teacher from the 1970's. His voice was deep, authoritative—someone used to giving orders. I would later learn that unlike the governor who ran for elective office the first chance he could, Jimenez preferred to be in the background—first as a member of the committee-to-elect, then as its chairman. He was behind the historic win of a House member who first ran as an Independent candidate. Until his victory, an Independent candidacy was considered a losing proposition. Then Jimenez masterminded the election victory of a former senator who had already lost twice in previous gubernatorial primaries. With Jimenez running the campaign, his candidate handily beat the then-incumbent lt. governor in the primary and went on to win the election. Four years later, however, Jimenez's candidate narrowly won in the primary only to lose to the current governor. But a year later, Jimenez was back on the hill after winning a Senate seat in a special election. A vacancy was created after the governor appointed one of the senators to a cabinet post. No one expected Jimenez to come out from where he was sulking and run for office for the first time in his political life. Since his candidate lost the gubernatorial election, he had been quiet and seldom seen in public. No one believed he could pull it off. But he campaigned tirelessly. Knocked on voters' doors. Shook their hands everywhere: at the church, the hospital, the supermarkets. He was there: at christenings, weddings, funerals, fiestas. He was generous. He said what he believed voters wanted to hear, and he said it well. It also helped that he had a large family and had doled out a lot of favors over the years when he was the former governor's right-hand man. The ruling party, moreover, underestimated Jimenez's chances. He won narrowly but convincingly. After he was sworn in, he declared that he would speak out against wrongdoing while encouraging policies beneficial to the people.

"So he's basically telling the governor he can 'get along' with the administration," Manny said.

The new administration had a rocky start— bumbling, really. But clean. And then it began to reek. Jimenez saw (smelled?) an opening and seized it—or was about to.

"What voters hate, perhaps more than anything else, is in-your-face government corruption," he told me.

I nodded as I took my tape recorder from my knapsack.

"No *lai*," Jimenez said. "Let's do this off the record first. I need to give you the background. The lay of the land."

He told me what I already knew, but then added, "Do you know that the governor's men are threatening to investigate me? I also know they have something against Sam. And probably you, too. I don't know with Manny. He's stuck-up that guy."

I said nothing. Jimenez looked at me as if studying my face. It was hard, on my part, not to look somewhere else.

"I'm not a thief," he finally said. "I don't steal from the government or the public."

In the previous administration, Jimenez was head of public works which signed off on millions of dollars of government contracts. "He didn't need to steal anything," Manny would later tell me. "But I bet he was offered a lot of 'gifts' — or 'loans.' "

"You probably know," Jimenez was now telling me, "that we charge and jail corrupt officials here." He was referring to the U.S. federal court. "But this governor is now inventing accusations against me."

"The Attorney General's Office?" I asked. It was under the governor's office.

"No, OPA," Jimenez said, referring to the Office of the Public Auditor. It was headed by an appointee of the governor, but the appointee was a lawyer/certified public accountant from the states and knew no one on island and wasn't related to anyone on Saipan. And it showed in his audit reports which were also beginning to displease the governor himself.

"But the governor can't tell OPA what to do," I said.

"It's the governor and his people who are feeding OPA with lies about me."

"But if they're lies—"

"Once you're accused publicly that's what the public will talk about."

"So—"

"So now turn on your recorder, and I will tell you about this administration's shenanigans."

70

S enator Jimenez read me an official letter he had already prepared and signed. It was addressed to the Senate president and the governor, and included in the file of official government communications available to reporters or anyone who would like a copy. In his letter, the senator did not make any accusations. But he mentioned each of the explosive allegations made by cabinet secretary Chuck Tolentino's wife in her sworn affidavit. "Are these true?" Jimenez asked, rhetorically, in his letter.

"I could have read this during session," Jimenez told me. "Privileged speech is how you call in the P.I."

"So—"

"But I want only you and your newspaper to get it because your outfit is trusted. You're locally owned. Sam has been here forever. And you guys are not for sale, right?" Jimenez smiled.

Hell no, I wanted to say. "No sir. But I'll have to get the governor's side."

"That's how it should be. Fair and balanced, right?"

"Yes sir."

"I've plenty more where that came from."

I walked toward the governor's office to talk with his public information officer, Jim. When he saw me, he said, "Oh come on."

"Yeah Jim. I've got to get your boss's comment."

"Man."

"It's from Jimenez."

Jim groaned.

"I don't think you should play poker."

"Screw you Benj."

So I told him what Jimenez just told me. I played back the tape. I also told Jim that the senator should have already sent a copy of the letter to the governor.

"This is bullshit Benj," Jim said. He didn't sound convincing.

"I'll call you again later," I said.

"You're not going to run this crap without our side of the story, right?"

"Fair and balanced."

"Right."

I drove back to the office. I told Manny about my interview and proceeded to write my story. I would just squeeze in later whatever comments I could get from the governor.

And then, of course, *Tun* Jack called. "*Lanya* my friend. I thought we are friends."

"We are sir."

"I thought we understood each other."

"We'll run a fair and balanced story and—"

"I'm so very, very disappointed." And he hung up. Did he just quote Marcos? That was what the Philippine president, about to be ousted, said when U.S. Senator Paul Laxalt told him, over the phone, to cut and cut cleanly.

Jim faxed a statement. He didn't pick up when I called his office. I completed my story. Read it twice. Printed a copy. Read it again. And then I submitted it to Manny who handed a copy to Sam.

"We're just doing our job," our publisher told us as he handed back the copy to Manny in the newsroom.

"All aboard," my editor said. Sam looked glum and said nothing.

71

THE story was the talk of the town. Guam's media sent their reporters to Saipan to get the story and any updates. The reporters from the other media outfits on Saipan swarmed Senator Jimenez's office, mainly to complain about his decision to give his letter to me alone. "Benjie was here," Jimenez told them, "none of you were—you snooze you lose."

"Do you think the governor's involved?" one of the reporters asked.

"In what?" Jimenez said.

"The allegation that Secretary Tolentino secretly met with one of the bidders."

"You'll have to ask the governor about that."

"Do you know where Mrs. Tolentino is?" asked another reporter.

"I believe she's off island."

I would later learn that Jimenez told her to leave the island the day before he met with me.

"Do you think it's proper that the highest elected official of the land is indebted to a group of investors who are doing business here or want to do so?"

"Good question," Jimenez replied, his face expressionless. I was quite sure he was enjoying the limelight.

"So what's next senator?"

"Will you call for the governor's impeachment?"

"What is your message to the governor?"

After professing his devotion to good governance and the good people of the islands he loved so much, the senator said he would ask his colleagues to conduct an oversight investigation. He said he would also ask the FBI to step in.

The reporters then rushed to the nearby administration building to get a comment from Governor Sanchez. But he wasn't around. Jim was, and he looked either sad or mad or both.

"The circus has come to town," he said as he stood in the lobby surrounded by reporters with their tape recorders thrust into his face like so many cups of hemlock.

"Is it true," one of the reporters said. He wasn't asking a question.

"You gotta be specific," Jim said.

"Was the governor involved in the attempt..."

"Alleged."

"...*alleged* attempt to 'fix' the bidding process for..."

"No, not true."

"Are you sure?"

"I won't even dignify that with..."

"Is the governor repaying his quote debt unquote to Japanese businessmen?"

"He..."

"Isn't that highly inappropriate for the governor to get a quote loan unquote from businessmen who deal with the government?"

"This governor is committed to transparency and good government."

"Do you really believe that?"

"You ought to be ashamed of yourself for asking that question."

"Aren't you ashamed yourself?"

And it went on and on, the questions which sounded more like denunciations while poor Jim stood there, his pale blue eyes behind his glasses like two small fish in a bowl. Flushed but not flustered, he even tried to smile now and then as he defended his boss.

"Like General Custer at Little Big Horn," Manny said as we watched the interview with Jim on cable TV later that evening.

"Poor Jim," I said.

"Good ol' Jim," Manny said. "He went down fighting."

I changed the topic. "When do we start on the Earhart story?"

"Sam's trying to get a hold of experts in the U.S. People who could authenticate what we have. Maybe get some DNA from the shirt."

"I'm actually excited."

"I'll ask Sam to OK an initial story about these new pieces of evidence—*potential* evidence—and just mention that we're also consulting experts, and that we'll run updates as we get new info."

"Maybe I should work on it right away."

"Go for it. The governor would be thankful for a new big story that could make people forget what they just learned today."

Before I left the office that night, I received a call from Weng. I almost giggled in moronic delight.

"This is not a social call," she said.

"So nice to hear your voice," I said.

"Jack's mad at you guys. Why?"

"Oh."

"Can I help fix it, whatever the mess is you created?"

"I'm touched."

"I'm serious."

"It's about the governor."

"Yeah, he was here earlier, and they talked in Chamorro, and they didn't sound happy."

"Where's the old man."

"They left."

"They'll get over it."

"What's happening anyway?"

"Long story. Can I see you?"

"Crazy."

"Is that a yes?

She sighed.

"Are you smiling?" I had to ask even though I was pretty sure she was.

72

THE next morning, I was in the office of my publisher, to take another look at the photos and the piece of clothing in the box. I was already writing my story. "I thought it was with you," Sam said, referring to the box. "Maybe it's with Manny?" Sam just looked at me. "I'm going to ask him," I said as Manny entered Sam's office. He looked at us. "What?" he asked.

"Is the Earhart box with you?" Sam asked.

"No," Manny said. He looked at the coffee table on which the box was placed the last time we were all in Sam's office.

Manny and I looked at Sam who, like us, was standing near the coffee table.

"I didn't bring it home," Sam said. "I left it here because I always lock that door," and he pointed to the door, "and Lulu," his secretary whose room was outside his, "double locks her door." Sam's office was a room within a room.

"And there was no sign of a break-in," Sam said.

"I was just about to ask you that," Manny said.

"Wait," I said. "The box is gone? Just like that?"

Sam said he asked his secretary if she noticed anything unusual with the door to their offices. She said she didn't notice anything. Sam also asked the production and circulation department folks—those on night shift—if they saw anyone who was not a newspaper employee in our building or anywhere near our building. No, they didn't.

"Should we call the cops?" I asked.

"And report what?" Manny asked.

"No sign of forcible entry," Sam said.

"But how can it just disappear like that?" I asked.

"The governor's men," Manny said.

"I bet our old friend Jack knows something," Sam said. "But that's all we have. Suspicion."

"Did you lose any of your keys?" Manny asked Sam.

"No I did not," our boss replied.

"What now?" I asked.

"I'm going to talk to the governor," Sam said.

"Benjie talk to Jack," Manny said.

The old man never gave me his number, so I went to see Weng instead at her workplace. She was now a cashier at one of the island's biggest supermarkets.

She looked happy and puzzled to see me. I wanted to hug her.

"Yes?" she said, smiling.

"How can I find Jack?"

Weng looked around, still smiling. "I told you. He's not in the best mood lately."

"I need to talk to him," I said.

"Go buy something and come back," she said. "My supervisor is looking at us. Don't look!"

I grabbed a can of soda from the cooler near her counter and handed it to her with a dollar bill.

"So?"

She looked at me, no longer smiling.

"God I miss you," I said despite myself.

"Hmmph."

"So where is the man of the hour?"

"He left early this morning."

"Who's your ride?"

"I drive now."

"Wow."

"Yeah."

"So we can run away now."

She chuckled. "He should be at the Japanese restaurant near the memorial park soon. I heard him mention it this morning. He's meeting with someone."

"When?"

"Today, lunch time."

It was 11:50 a.m. "Can I see you again later?" I asked.

"Go."

"Later," I said.

She sighed.

73

IHAVE nothing to say to you mister," *Tun* Jack said when he saw me in the parking lot of the restaurant. We arrived at about the same time. "*Tun* Jack, the box is gone," I sputtered. He was trying to walk fast, but then he stopped and looked at me.

"The Earhart box?" he asked.

"Yeah."

He shook his head. "So you think I took it?" His graying eyebrows were raised.

"Did you?"

"*Lanya*, are you accusing me?"

"No sir, but…"

"It's you guys who can't be trusted." He started walking away again.

"But who else would want to get that box?" I said.

He spoke in Chamorro as he entered the restaurant. The only word I caught was *diablo*. Devil.

Back at the office, Sam told me that the governor wasn't returning his calls. My publisher also just learned that the government was canceling two printing jobs, the contracts for which were earlier awarded to our newspaper's printing department.

"And Rev and Tax just called. They want to review some of our financial records," Sam said, referring to the Division of Revenue and Taxation,

"Can they do that?" Manny asked. The three of us were in Sam's office.

"They're already doing it," Sam said.

"Shouldn't we fight back?" Manny asked.

"What Manny said," I said looking at Sam who looked, at that moment, detached, like a condemned man who had already made peace with his fate.

"Now, now," he said. "We'll take things one at a time, as they happen. And we'll continue to do our job which is to keep this community informed. But right now, I've got to talk with my wife."

In the editorial room, Manny and I didn't talk about the sudden crisis bedeviling our employer—and therefore, our jobs. I wrote a follow-up story on the scandals involving the administration which Manny placed on the front page.

"I'll blast them on the editorial page," Manny told me.

I wanted to see Weng. But she didn't want me to call her at their house. I also didn't know their number. It was past 8, and I wasn't sure if Sweet was home. We were already like old couples who had been married for decades. We had become more like room-mates than man and wife. Back in the day, which wasn't really that long ago, we really wanted to have a baby, and we tried real hard, and went at it, well, religiously. It seemed that we couldn't make it happen. So we had given up. Now and then, we still went through the motions, but they were mostly perfunctory.

Lately, she had been coming home late. 9 or 10. She said she had joined a bowling league. She said I should drop by at the bowling center. I never did. Looking back, I should have because it might have saved me a lot of grief later on.

74

HE next day, I was in the office of Senator Jimenez. I was hoping to get more damning—to the administration—quotes from him. "He wants to see you," his secretary told me as I stepped into their reception area. "He's waiting for you," she added, looking at the door to his office. He was at his desk, reading our newspaper.

"Senator," I said.

"Pull up a chair," he said.

"Anything new?"

"At 1 p.m. today—you have a camera right?"

I showed him the office-issued camera that was in my knapsack.

"At 1 p.m., go to the poker arcade just beside the store two blocks from here, going south."

"What's going on?"

"The governor's special assistant for budget, *si* Lisa, will be there, gambling. Not during but after her lunch break. She's usually there all afternoon on weekdays."

"Really?"

"Go there, take her photo. And ask her to explain herself."

"Wow."

"Yeah *lai*. Wow. Your governor is running a circus."

"Can I quote on you on that?"

"No. Not yet."

"Darn."

"Anyway," Jimenez said, "how are you guys holding up?"

"What do you mean sir?"

"I know this governor is applying pressure on you guys. He has something on Sam."

"I don't know anything about that."

"Did the governor's people offer anything yet to you and your editor?"

"I, uh…"

"I know your publisher could be in trouble. But he has to stand firm for the sake of good government. I ought to call him. But I know he doesn't like me."

"I, uh…"

"He's a former Peace Corps volunteer, your publisher, when he first got here. Most haoles who decided to settle down want us natives to remain backward, and for our island to remain in the jungle. They think we're ridiculous for aping western ways, and that we should stick to wearing a loincloth, drinking coconut wine, fishing and paddling canoes. They don't want their paradise-island marred by brown people acting like the white people they're trying to avoid or they thought they've left behind in the states. They think our potholed roads were quaint. That tin houses were comfy. When I was a young man during the Trust Territory days, this haole lady, wife of a TT official, told my mother we were 'lucky' not to have a washing machine and a dryer, and that we were 'blessed' with tropical winds which she said was way better for drying newly washed clothes. We also didn't have indoor plumbing back in the day. But I don't recall any haole envying us for squatting in an outhouse. I keep telling them, we Chamorros are not like the other islanders who want to remain islanders. Yes we want to be Chamorros and chew betel nut and eat fruit bats, but we want to sail our own yacht when we go fishing, and we want a concrete home, and we want our kids studying in college in the U.S. We want electricity and phones and computers and airplanes and modern stores and restaurants and washing machines and dryers. And what's wrong with that? You want to remain native? Nothing wrong with that. Go up north, to one of the Northern Islands. Stay there. Enjoy nature. Fish all you want. The fish there die of old age, you know. Wild pigs, I was told, will approach you. They're mellow. Because they eat the marijuana planted there, probably by Peace Corps volunteers like your boss, years ago. Hahahaha. Anyway, you want to go native, go ahead. But many of us just want a comfortable life, what these haoles are so used to, they take it for granted. But Sam, your boss, he's unlike most Americans who have settled down here. He has mellowed over the years. He used to be a radical, a hippie. Well, most of us were in those days. Anyway, I know you guys are trying to be fair, and I hope you'll stay fair, because *lanya* I've got plenty more information to share with you."

"Like what sir?"

"Go take pictures of the budget lady at the poker arcade. Then we'll talk again tomorrow. But remember: don't tell anyone I'm your source. I'll deny it."

THERE she was. The only customer, which wasn't surprising. It was early afternoon on a weekday. She wore a long blue skirt and a white blouse. Her back to the door, she didn't see me enter. She was punching the buttons on the video poker machine. She was also smoking beside the NO SMOKING sign posted on a wall on which a clock was also showing the time: 1:15 p.m. It was as if I just died and went to news-photography heaven. I took out my camera, and approached her quietly. I aimed for her profile—my photo must show that it was her, the governor's budget official gambling on government time, and smoking, too, in a no-smoking area. I took several photos, and the sound my camera made startled her. She managed to hear it despite the jangly music, loud beeps and chimes emitted by the gluttonous gambling device that had gripped her full attention. I continued to take photos. Her face, eyes wide, eyebrows raised, now turned to the camera.

"Hey!" she said.

"Hi ma'am!" I said still clicking away.

"Hey stop that!" She was frowning now, but she remained seated on her padded stool.

"Any comments ma'am?" I took out my notebook and ballpen.

"What the hell is that about?" she asked. "And who the hell are you?"

"I'm a reporter," I said.

"I have nothing to say," she said, looking at me as if I were a drunk who just staggered into church during Mass.

"Ma'am you're gambling during government work hours," I said.

"I just got here. I was waiting for the owner. I'm conducting a survey of small businesses."

"Can I quote you?"

"No! I don't want to talk to you, and you better not put those photos in the paper. Are with you the *Times*?"

"Yes ma'am."

"Sam is my uncle. His wife is my cousin. You can't do this to me."

"Just doing my job ma'am." I walked toward the exit. "Please call me at our office if you've changed your mind and want to say something on the record."

She was at the office later that day, pleading with Sam not to run the story. She said she had nothing to do with the ongoing audit of our newspaper and the cancelation of printing orders. She said Sam should give her another chance.

Sam said he sympathized with her, and assured her that his "troubles" with her governor had nothing to do with the story I filed. In fact, he added, he didn't even know that we were running the story until she showed up in his office.

Sam, in short, told her the truth. He then, gently, told her to remain strong, and that "all things shall pass." She then demanded to talk to her aunt, Sam's wife. So he gave have her his wife's phone number. Later, in the art room, Sam took a good look at the page 1 image on the computer. Manny blew up the photo I had taken. It was a great photo. The budget official was looking at the camera: she held her cigarette in her left hand, her right hand appeared to be pressing the buttons of the video poker machine. The NO SMOKING sign was visible and so was the time on the wall clock.

"Like a drawing," Sam said, chuckling. "Drawing" was the term in the P.I. for news photos that were deliberately set up to make them look more "interesting."

The following day, it was the biggest news story. Even some of the governor's allies in the Legislature grumbled at what they described as "amateur hour" at the executive branch. But no one, not even Jimenez, wanted to go on record and criticize the budget official. However, many members of the local community sent angry letters to the editor demanding the resignation of the budget official. Some said the governor ought to fire her. Otherwise, they said, he should resign himself.

"Ready for your next assignment?" Senator Jimenez told me over the phone.

I said yes. He instructed me to meet one of his staffers at the legislative building just before lunch-time.

"More explosive stuff," Jimenez said.

76

THE governor's nephew, the son of his brother, who worked at a government agency had embezzled over $30,000 in public funds. The nephew was addicted to video poker and, quite possibly, to crystal meth. When the agency director learned about it, he told the governor, who was, naturally, livid. He and his brother managed to raise $30,000 which was then returned to the agency. The nephew was banished to the states.

"Ask the governor about it," Jimenez told me. "Ask his brother. Ask the agency director. Ask the attorney general. File an Open Government Act request. Do all the things that a reporter is supposed to do."

"Why do you hate us so much?" Jim, the governor's spokesman, told me over the phone when he finally returned my many calls.

"Just doing my job Jim."

"Whose feeding you this bullshit? Jimenez?"

"Is it true or not?"

"That you're allowing yourself and your newspaper to be used as a battering-ram by a sleazy politician who wants to run for governor?"

"Jim calm down."

"Don't tell me to calm down. I'm calm!" he shouted.

I was also working on the Amelia Earhart story. I told Manny I would write about the photos and the piece of clothing, and about *Tun* Jack and the disappearance of the box when we began reporting things that the administration considered unpleasant.

"All-out war," Sam said when Manny and I told him about it. "Well, you may fire when you are ready gentlemen."

I learned from Manny, that Sam and his wife were barely speaking. Apparently, she believed that we were acting like Jimenez's puppets. She didn't like the senator although he was a cousin (the governor was also a cousin).

When I finally got a hold of *Tun* Jack—in the lobby of the administration building; he was about to leave—I told him about my Earhart story.

"I can't tell you what to do *lai*, but if you gonna' write about things you no longer have, please don't mention me. You saw an old, faded photo of someone who looked like a Caucasian woman, and you'll most likely end up repeating old hearsay and speculation. But then again, you and your newspaper are into fiction, right?"

Elections were a few months away. The good news, and there was plenty about the state of the economy and additional funding for popular public services and programs—these were shoved aside by the follow-up stories and letters to the editor and other commentaries that depicted the administration as a den of bumbling thieves.

But no one in the executive branch, even off-the-record, wanted to confirm the key details of the embezzling nephew's story.

"They're scared to death," Jimenez told me. "This involves obstruction of justice—an impeachable offense. Maybe I should write an official letter to the governor, to the Senate president and the House speaker."

Two days later, Jimenez told me to meet him in his office. There, he showed me the letter. It was written on the Legislature's official letterhead and addressed to the governor. It was a public document and it "asked" the governor several pointed and rhetorical questions about the gubernatorial nephew who embezzled public funds.

"You make a news story about it," the senator told me, "but I will also run it as paid advertising in your paper."

I told the governor's office about the letter. The governor's spokesman, Jim, faxed a one-page statement denying that the governor committed any wrongdoing while decrying Senator Jimenez's "politics of destruction through smears" that our newspaper "is shamelessly, indecently, irresponsibly peddling."

It got uglier. The governor's brother, speaking for his son, said he would sue us for libel. Manny, with Sam's tacit approval, wrote one thunderous editorial after the other. Senator Jimenez quoted the editorials every time he was interviewed by reporters. One of the governor's loyal supporters among the lawmakers told me to tell Sam to "watch out." I asked him if he was threatening my employer. "No *lai*, I'm just saying that people who live in glass houses shouldn't throw stones. Tell him I said so."

So I told Sam who nodded his head, sadly, it seemed.

77

I SOON learned that my publisher's marriage was crumbling. The governor's men had told Sam's wife and/or closest relatives about Sam's supposed "infidelities." "Is that true?" I asked Manny, who shrugged his shoulders. I likewise learned from Sweet that her employer had already "advised" her that her contract might not be renewed. Manny and I suspected that the governor's men were also pressuring Sweet's employer to let her go. "Shouldn't we raise more hell?" I asked Manny. He shrugged his shoulders, again. His wife worked as office manager and accountant for a local company that owned apartments on island. Her boss, too, was vulnerable to political pressure. "She's probably next," Manny said.

I continued working on my Amelia Earhart story. That night while driving home, I suddenly remembered the old Amelia Earhart-related news clippings that Rob, over the phone earlier that day, said I could borrow and photocopy so I headed to his house which was along the way. It was past 9 already, and he seemed somewhat startled to see me.

"Hey," he said, before adding loudly, "Benjie!" He was shirtless and in his boxer shorts.

"The clippings, can I get them now?"

"Oh. I thought you wanted me to bring them to you. You should have called man."

"Well I'm here."

He had not asked me to come in which irritated me. He stood behind the door, holding it as if preparing to slam it if I dared enter.

"Can I come in?" I finally asked.

"Huh? Uh, you want to come in?"

"Dude what's wrong with you?"

"Come in, come in, I was just…"

"You've got company?"

"No! No! Plop yourself on the sofa and I'll, I'll…" And he walked hurriedly to his bedroom.

He's with someone, I told myself.

"So who's the victim?" I asked him as he handed me a folder filled with newspaper clippings.

"What?" he said as he looked behind him, at the bedroom door.

"Who's the girl?"

"What? Please be careful with these," he said, referring to the clippings as he walked toward the front-door.

"I'll return them to you as soon as I photo-copy them tomorrow," I said as I stepped out.

"All right, see you."

"Man you're in a hurry."

He slammed the door.

Sweet wasn't home yet, but there was a cup of instant Japanese noodles and soda crackers on our dining table, so no problem. I was still eating when she arrived. She looked rattled.

"What's the matter?" I asked.

"Nothing."

"Did you eat already?"

"Yeah," and she went into the restroom.

She had her own "world" now, peopled with her own friends, and they did their own thing. I didn't mind. I had work to do—and Weng and I had become, as she would put it, "phone pals." We also had been seeing each other whenever her husband was on the neighboring islands. Later that week, Sweet told me she was pregnant.

78

I WASN'T *that* surprised. We still performed the, well, horizontal mambo now and then, perhaps twice a month. Sweet, however, seemed unhappy—or upset—about her new condition. I assumed it was because her contract wasn't going to be renewed.

Meanwhile, while the local political storm our newspaper helped create raged on, I continued drafting my Amelia Earhart story. I carefully read and re-read Rob's newspaper clippings which I had photo-copied.

Death affects people—especially famous people—differently. They are transformed into apparitions that could walk among us. Amelia disappeared, and so she's now somewhere or everywhere. Many people claimed that they saw her, or talked to people who did. Why would they lie, these witnesses? Did they perhaps misremember? But where are the solid proofs? The photo we saw was badly faded, although the Caucasian person in it looked like Amelia. But when was it taken, and where?

After the war her husband, George Putnam, visited Saipan and met many people and asked them questions about what they knew or what they had heard about an American lady pilot. But he never learned anything that led him to believe Amelia had been on the island. He was an indefatigable publicist, known to have faked death threats against himself just to create a buzz about his latest book project. Yet he never wrote about the possibility that

Amelia was captured by the Japanese and brought to Saipan.

In an Amelia Earhart biography published in 1989—it's reputedly the best of the lot—the author declared that "the theory that Amelia was a spy is now almost dead. The welter of documents released by the U.S. government and those available in the Roosevelt Library at Hyde Park must convince all but the most cynical researcher that there was no covert operation involved in Amelia's disappearance."

And yet…

As I write this, absolutely no one can definitely say what exactly happened to Amelia Earhart and Fred Noonan—which means anything could have happened to them. For example, she could have run out of fuel and died either during the emergency landing at sea or shortly afterward. Which is like saying that a frustrated Marxist manqué dying for attention, and acting alone, shot and killed JFK. How very dull indeed. But unlike JFK's assassination, which is, by now, an open-and-shut case (yes, a nutcase did it), Amelia's disappearance still fuels an ongoing debate.

I decided not to write a straight news article. It would be a feature story written in the first person. A brief introduction to the story of Amelia's disappearance and theories about it, the ongoing search for any evidence, and my encounter with a local man who showed me a photo that could possibly be of Amelia taken on Saipan while she was a captive here, and a piece of clothing that might have belonged to her. Unfortunately, I would add, someone snatched them away, and the "theft" incident could be politically motivated. I wouldn't mention names. Or should I?

Manny said I should tell *Tun* Jack about the story I was writing—as a courtesy. But the old man was, at the time, shuttling between the neighboring islands of Rota and

Tinian, "fixing" things for his political party. Weng, who was now driving her own car, would meet me at night, on a beach somewhere. She advised me to meet her husband in person on a weekday at the governor's office. She would tell me when. She didn't expect him to be back anytime soon.

"What exactly is he doing on Rota and Tinian anyway?" I asked.

"I never ask. But it's work-related. He's always talking to the governor on the phone."

"So how's married life?"

"How's yours?'

"I asked first."

She sighed. "Sometimes I think he married me out of pity."

"What? And not because you're oozing with sex appeal?"

"Shut up. Well, he doesn't seem interested in, you know, intimacy."

"Come on."

"He likes hugging, and kissing me on the forehead and cheeks."

"I don't want to hear it."

"It's like he basically adopted me. And I'm his ward."

"What if he's seeing someone else?

"I wish. Maybe. I don't know."

"Jealous?"

"What happens if I get pregnant?"

It was as if someone had grabbed me by the shoulders, shook me and was yelling at my face. Suddenly, I remembered that I had not told Weng that Sweet was carrying child. Mine.

"Are you?" I finally said.

"I'm getting a pregnancy kit tomorrow."

"OK."

"Is your wife pregnant?"

I said nothing, and thought hard about my answer—which pretty much answered her question.

"Great," she said. "Did you ever plan on telling me? Did you actually think I wouldn't know anyway?"

I didn't know what to say. I heard her sigh. I couldn't look at her. We were in my car, sipping soda. I knew she was looking at me, hard, like Medusa.

"So what's next Mr. Benjie," which was what she called me when she was pissed.

"Are you pregnant?"

"Three months delayed. And your wife?"

I still could not reply to that question.

"I wanna go home now," she said.

79

I MET with *Tun* Jack the following week. Or rather, I ran after him in the parking lot outside the governor's office. He still didn't seem thrilled to see me. He looked at me as if he expected me to say something unspeakably stupid. I told him about the article I was writing. I said I was seeking his permission to mention him as the source of the now lost photo and clothing that probably belonged to Amelia Earhart.

"You have nothing, and I don't want anything to do with whatever it is you're doing," he said before driving away.

I finished my article and handed it to Manny.

"Sounds like you're whining," he told me after reading it.

I could feel my face redden. "Will you run it?"

Manny looked at me. "I'll ask Sam."

But lately, our publisher was never around. We assumed he was trying to save his marriage—or quicken its unraveling.

Manny himself seemed distracted—or indifferent. In the past few days, his editorials were about everything else but the scandals hounding the governor and his administration.

"I'll run it," Manny said, referring to my article. "But without your innuendoes."

"My what?"

"We should stop kicking the hive. Enough already."

I assumed he was talking about the governor. "Whatever," I said before walking out of the room.

Manny published it on the op-ed page. He also published letters that ridiculed me for writing it.

"Can I at least reply?" I asked Manny.

"Make it short," he snapped.

Manny had changed, and had become more taciturn and abrupt than he was before. He didn't even tell me that he was headed to Manila for a week-long vacation. He asked for two weeks, but I learned that Sam told Manny that a week should be enough. Sam took over as acting editor. He was even more morose than Manny.

A week later, Manny was back, and he told he was quitting.

"What?" I asked. "Why? What?" I asked again.

"You'll get my job."

"I don't want it," I said, and probably believed it, too, at the time.

"The wife and I got our U.S. visas. We're going to California."

"For good?"

"I hope so."

"Why?"

"I'll be 45 soon. Time to try something new."

"Why?"

"We're tired of island life."

"What will you do in California?"

"I don't know. Maybe become a caregiver."

I would later learn from the governor's spokesman, Jim, that it was the governor who wrote a letter addressed to the U.S. Embassy in Manila that Manny and his wife showed the American consul when they applied for a U.S. visa.

"And what can we do for you my friend?" Jim inquired.

I laughed and didn't say anything. On the same day, Weng said she was carrying my child and Sweet said she wanted a divorce.

80

I DIDN'T know whether to be glad or sad. It was headed there, of course; Sweet and I separating. I was, in a way, glad that she initiated the process. But what about our child? I asked her. We were at the beach near the memorial park, seated on sand. It was Friday, early evening. The sun had already, and spectacularly, set. There were families of tourists in the lagoon, but there was no one else near us. We didn't want to talk about what we had to talk about at the barracks. The walls there didn't have ears; they were connected to a public announcement system. At the beach, I looked at the bleeding horizon and drank diet Pepsi from a can. No beer for me. I wanted to be as sober as possible. Sweet was sipping bottled water. It seemed that she didn't want to look at me.

"What about the baby?" I asked her again, looking at her profile. She was as pretty as ever.

"Promise me you won't get mad," she said.

"I won't get mad. Wait. Why should I get mad?"

"I am pregnant."

"Yeah, I know."

"You're not the father."

I could feel the blood rushing to my face, and my hands became suddenly clammy. I couldn't breathe. It was like a sudden asthma attack.

"Benj are you OK?" she said, her left hand on my right shoulder. I was breathing furiously. I wanted to lash out at her. I wanted to yell at her. I wanted one of us to drown in the lagoon right there and then.

"How could you do that?" I asked. *To me*, I wanted to add.

"I'm sorry." She was teary eyed now. "Really sorry." As if she just accidentally stepped on my foot. I thought about telling her *my* truth—Weng and *her* pregnancy. But I stopped myself. I wanted her to feel profoundly sorry for me. I wanted her to feel guilty. I wanted her to believe that I was devastated more than I was. I was actually deeply insulted.

"Who's the asshole?"

"Don't say that."

"Do I know him?"

She hesitated before nodding.

"I can't believe this," I said. "Why?" Of course I knew why. It was over between us. It had been over a long time ago. She just made it official.

"Who is he?" I asked again.

"Does it matter?"

"Depends."

She looked at me.

"No. I won't do anything stupid. I don't want to go to jail. I just want to know. That's all. You have disgraced me. I will be a laughing stock. The cuckold. I just want to know who crapped on my head."

She was still looking at me.

"Whatever," I said. "So how many months now?"

"What?"

"Your pregnancy."

She just looked at me again. Of course she didn't want to tell me. I might do the math and figure it out.

"Fine," I said.

"What now?" she said.

"You have a lawyer?"

"What?"

"For the divorce."

"Oh. Yes, I think so."

"You think so? Well, go ahead. You want a divorce, you get a lawyer. And I'll just sign the papers."

"I'm moving out."

"Sure."

"I'm sorry."

"I'm sorry, too."

She held my hand. I wanted to pull it away.

81

BEFORE I could tell Weng about the, well, "good news," she informed me that her suspicion had just been confirmed. Her husband was seeing someone else. "Who?" I asked. Correction, she said. The old man was seeing other *women*. There were two or even more, she added.

One of them, apparently ignoring *Tun* Jack's instructions, tried to reach him by phone at his house. He wasn't around and she ended up talking with Weng who, with the instinct known only to wives, introduced herself as his niece—the wife of one of his nephews. "Who's calling," Weng asked the woman, a Filipina, who said her name was Mila, and that she was already at the airport. She said she just arrived from Tinian, and Jack was supposed to pick her up. Then the woman blurted out, "He's here now, thank you!" And hung up.

Weng said she didn't want to ask her husband about Mila, whoever the hell she was. (At this point, I was thinking, No, that Mila can't be Rob's on-and-off girlfriend, Mila.)

Weng said she also found a carefully folded piece of paper in a pocket of one of the old man's pants that she had to bring to the Laundromat. She recognized the handwriting—his. And he had written the name of a woman, Alma, and her telephone number. It was a Rota phone number.

"But they could be anyone, Mila and Alma," I said.

"I talked to them," Weng replied.

"And they admitted that they were seeing your husband?"

"No silly. I pretended to be someone else, and I learned that he sees them now and then."

"He sees a lot of people."

"I know what I know."

"Well, who cares."

"I don't."

I then told her the "good news." Instead of expressing elation, or at least a hint of it, Weng said, "She has been seeing your haole friend, a lot."

"Who?"

"The only haole friend of yours I've met so far."

"Rob." My infernal blood, like hounds unleashed, rushed to my face. My ears felt like they were burning.

"How do you know?" I asked, almost choking.

"I saw them together in a restaurant. When they saw me they suddenly looked embarrassed about being seen together."

"When was this?"

"A few days ago I think."

"That's all you saw?"

"I think I saw enough."

"Why didn't you tell me?"

"I'm telling you now. "

"She is pregnant, and it's not mine."

Weng said nothing.

"I will divorce her, and we can be together now, openly, finally. You've got to divorce the old man."

"Just like that," she said. "Signatures on official documents and that's it."

I was getting pissed, and not just about learning that it was Rob, of all people, who was banging my wife, but that the woman I loved didn't sound like she wanted to be with me now that we could be officially a couple.

"I hate to ask this question," I said, trying not to scream, "but do you still want to be with me?"

She looked at me like I was the most pitiful creature on the face of the planet.

82

OW, I thought, would it be when Weng and I were together all or most of the time? I was lying in bed, alone in the room that my wife and I had shared for over a year, in an apartment unit where we had methodically, irrevocably bored each other. I loved Sweet, of course. And I was pretty sure she loved me, too. Yet our relationship unraveled precisely when we were left alone with one another. Familiarity didn't breed contempt in our case. It resulted in indifference.

Would Weng and I end in the same emotional *cul de sac*? How would it be when there was no longer the element of the forbidden in our relationship—when there was no need to hide anymore or to lie, except to one another. With Sweet in the beginning, her quirks were cute; eventually they became irritants. The way she used her spoon when she should be using a fork. She liked carrots which I hated—and those Filipino fish dishes that even as a kid I considered too fishy with that raw, blood-salty, rusty-metallic taste; almost as disgusting as raw oysters which felt like globs of green phlegm on my tongue. She liked oysters.

And where would we stay, Weng and I? I was pretty sure she didn't want to move into someone else's love nest. Jesus. What a phrase.

She had to tell the old man that she wanted a divorce. Then we could move into another apartment, and perhaps get married eventually. We would have a child. I would be a father. In my room, the air-con was on but I was suddenly perspiring.

At the office the following day, our publisher Sam met with me and his two other reporters, Noel and Joel, in his room to announce that Manny had left for the states, and might not return to the island.

"I'll be taking over," Sam said. "We're going to hire a new reporter. Benjie will be my assistant."

I could feel Noel and Joel giving me a quick glance.

"We will continue as before," Sam said. "We will not bow before the powers-that-be. Our job is to inform this community, not to kiss anyone's butt. Questions?"

Noel, Joel and I looked at each other.

"My wife will remain associate publisher. She's still on board. You may have heard that the governor and his people are trying to drive a wedge between me and Mrs. Cohen. They've failed. My wife and I are in this together. The newspaper, the business, is still under pressure, but we'll keep doing what we're doing."

Sam and I had a separate one-on-one meeting.

"Can you be my editor?" he asked.

"Of course," I said, of course.

He looked me. "Do you want to be my editor?"

I nodded, but probably not as enthusiastically as Sam hoped.

"Manny spoke highly of you."

"He's a good editor."

"They bought him out."

I didn't say anything.

"They think all of us can be bought."

I absent-mindedly looked at my palms.

"Anyway," Sam said, "once the new reporter arrives you'll be the new editor."

"Oh," I said.

"Oh?"

"I mean, yes sir, thanks."

At that point in my life, what the hell did I want? So many things were happening to me and around me at the same time. It reminded me of that day on the beach in a province north of Manila. My old newspaper, *The Daily World,* was holding a company-paid outing; Lenten season. The sea—the South China Sea—was almost black, with the waves suddenly emerging and rushing toward the shore. My co-workers and I stood in the waist-deep water, but if you failed to hop at the right time as the waves rolled toward you, they would drag you to the shore like a crash-test-dummy. And as you rolled over and over, gasping for air, hearing nothing but thuds and the sea in your ears, and seeing nothing but flashing images as if you were in a dark room and someone was playing with the light switch—all the while you'd wonder if it would ever end, your whirling and twirling, and you would be relieved when it finally did, and horrified at the same time at how helpless you were as Mother Nature repeatedly bitch-slapped you.

When I became a reporter, I wanted to rise through the ranks until I become the editor-in-chief. I did not just wish it. I worked hard to be ready for it—to deserve it. I never stopped learning the tricks of the trade—and the latest trends in my chosen profession. Manny was a good teacher. He taught me by example. After a year, I was pretty sure I was ready to succeed him. But now I was in a middle of some pretty intense personal shit, as that asshole Rob would put it. I needed to sort things out. First with Sweet. Finalize that goddamn divorce. Then Weng. Meaning, I had to talk with her husband. But did I need to? Should I? Maybe Weng could just tell him she was leaving him.

I wish Manny was still around.

83

I'M calling you first because you're my friend," Senator Jimenez said over the phone. I was about to leave the office and head to Capital Hill. "I'm having a press conference. Actually we're having a joint press conference. We. The governor and I."

That was one of the last things I thought I would hear in my lifetime. But Manny would not have been as startled as I was. Politics, he once told me, could be the only human endeavor in which nothing is impossible.

"It's time to move beyond petty politics," the senator said. "We must move forward. I have agreed to be the governor's running mate."

What could I possibly say to that?

"Mr. Benjie are you still there," the senator asked.

"Uh, yes sir, uh…"

He chuckled. "I know it's a bit surprising."

"Uh…" A *bit*?

"But the welfare of this great commonwealth is more important than politics," he said

I could, of course, have said at this point, "Are you and the governor out of your minds? After what you've been saying about each other, now you're suddenly a team? Do you actually think voters are that stupid?"

Instead, I asked: "But what about the lt. governor?"

"Don't tell anyone I told you, but he's going to be appointed to the local Supreme Court. He's a former judge after all. Anyway, I'm telling you all this because I want you to be the first to know. Also the governor and I can use the talents of a good reporter like you."

"Oh."

He chuckled again. "I'll see you at the press conference."

Weng also called. "I told him," she said.

"OK," I said, relieved and anxious at the same time. What now? I thought.

"He wants to talk to you," Weng said.

"Is he mad?"

"He's not happy."

"Did he hurt you or threaten to—"

"Don't be silly."

"So why does he want to talk to me?"

"Are you scared?"

"Are you nuts?"

"I'm about to hang up."

"No! I'm sorry, I uh—"

"You never talked to me like that before."

"I know, I'm really sorry—

"You should talk to him."

"I, uh, what for?"

"I don't know, but I'm dumping him for you and the least we can do is show some respect. He's an old man and he treated me well."

"Hah."

"He took care of me. He's been kind to me. Up to now."

I was getting increasingly pissed. "Then maybe," but I bit my tongue.

"What?"

I bit my tongue again. So this, I thought, is maturity. Not saying stupid things out loud. Who infected me with maturity?

"Talk to him please," Weng said. "Let's get this done and over with it." Pause. "I want us to be together."

I closed my eyes. God, I did want us to be together. "Okay," I said.

I met the old man in his office at the administration building. "I don't need an office," he told me as I sat in one of the two chairs in front of his desk, "but the governor insists, and he's the boss." It was a small room, but the furniture looked shiny and new. On his desk were a fax machine and a phone. The white walls were still bare except for the framed official photo of the governor behind *Tun* Jack's black executive chair.

"I wanted to start over," he said, staring at me with his shrewd rabbit eyes. He looked tired but alert. "I wanted us to be friends again. You've probably heard about Senator Jimenez's decision to set politics aside and work with the governor."

"For the betterment of the commonwealth," I said before I could stop myself.

Tun Jack chuckled. "You're starting to sound like your editor—your *former* editor. Congratulations. Sam, for sure, will name you the new editor."

"I don't know, but thank you."

"As I said, I wanted to forget our previous, you know, disagreements and move forward."

It was as if I were hearing one of the governor's stump speeches.

"But then," the old man said, "*this*." And he made a gesture with his hands as if showing me a mess I left on his table.

"I should feel insulted," he added. "Disrespected." He looked at me as if I had to be pitied.

"You were seeing other women," I said. In my mind, I had just kicked him off the high moral ground.

The old man smiled. "That's what she said?"

"It's true isn't it?"

"I'm not here to argue with you young man. But you obviously don't know what you're talking about."

"Sure."

"Ask Weng. Ask the others if I were…what's the word? A lecher. You don't know me. You think you do but you don't."

I just looked at him, unemotionally I hoped.

"I married Weng so she didn't need to work as a dancer in a club. I like her. There are two other young women, Filipinas also, I'm helping out. They quit their jobs because they don't like their employers, but they don't want to go back to P.I."

"Will you marry them too?"

Tun Jack laughed. "Will you marry Weng?" he said.

"Of course."

"And then leave her if you see someone new?"

"Of course not."

"Yet you were cheating on your fiancée before she got here, and you were still seeing Weng even though she and you were married to someone else."

I was tumbling down from the high moral ground. "I don't know what you're talking about."

"I may be old, but my eyesight is still pretty good."

"My wife left me—"

"She's not stupid either."

"Look—"

"As I've said, I don't want to argue with you, and I want to settle this once and for all."

"I'm marrying Weng."

"I won't divorce her."

"We don't care. We'll get a lawyer. I'll put it in the paper. The governor's henchman—"

"Hah."

"—his young wife and young or younger girlfriends…"

"Not if we kick you off the island first."

"And I can write about that, too."

He was no longer smiling. "We'll shut down your newspaper."

"Good luck with that."

"Or ask Sam to fire you."

"There are other newspapers on island—you can't shut them all down. And I can fax my story from Manila."

"I never thought you were stupid."

"Thanks, I guess."

"And the *Times* is more useful to us alive than dead."

I was beginning to despise the old man.

"Let's be friends again," he said.

I said nothing.

"I believe I have other information about Amelia Earhart that you'll find interesting. I think I've got other photos and other pieces of evidence…"

"And what you do want in return?"

"You staying away from my wife."

"No way."

"You're young. Not bad looking. Plenty fish in the ocean."

"We love each other."

"You think you do, now. Then the rest of your lives will happen to the both of you. It may not be pretty."

"How can you know that? How can anyone possibly know that?"

"How can you be sure it won't happen to you?"

"Just leave us alone please."

"I'll leave you alone if you leave my wife alone."

"She wants to be with me."

"Tell her you've changed your mind, and you could become a famous reporter—the one who solved the mystery of Amelia Earhart's disappearance."

"I don't—"

"Think about it first. Think long and hard about it."

84

MY second-grade teacher, impressed with my reading skills, told me and my mother that I should read the dictionary. My mom and I took my teacher's advice literally. My mother bought a pocket dictionary and I read each entry before giving up on page 4. It was boring. There was no "story." And I eventually realized that my teacher could not have possibly expected a 7-year-old to read the entire dictionary even if it's the pocket version. So what did she mean when she said I should read the dictionary? Or did we mishear her? Perhaps she said, "He probably reads the dictionary."

And why was I thinking, of all things, about that episode from my childhood when I was faced with a life-changing, possibly insoluble dilemma?

I wanted to be a playwright. In 10th grade I had an idea for a play—about a narcissist serial killer. He killed men who were better looking than he was. The play went nowhere because I didn't know how the story would unfold. Two years later, I had another idea for yet another play. A holding cell for the souls of those headed to purgatory. My main characters were a tranny and a leftist activist. Again, it eventually ran out of gas, sputtered and died in the middle of the road to nowhere.

I couldn't write a play. So I decided to be a newspaper writer, primarily because, unlike playwriting, it involved getting regular paychecks. I would be a reporter to improve my writing skills, learn new things, like maturity, and parlay them into works of art: i.e. creative writing. Perhaps short stories, a novel or two or even a play. Get published. Win awards. Get laid a lot.

What I ended up doing were a lot of news stories and all-around hack work. But I tried to be good at it. I liked my job. I could not imagine doing anything else. And now I was on the verge of achieving two major career goals, one of which I didn't even imagine possible: assuming the top editorial post in a newspaper, and becoming the journalist who would reveal to the entire world the solution to the one of the 20th century's greatest mysteries.

All I had to do was ditch the woman I loved—who was already married.

However—my favorite word—the editor's job was mine already, and with or without physical evidence I could conduct my own investigation so I could still write a blockbuster news story about Amelia Earhart. Right?

I was quite sure, in any case, that if I deprived myself of Weng's company I would crave it like a fish in a kitchen sink, day-dreaming about the ocean.

Should I tell Sam? But this concerned my personal life.

At the office, I merely stared at the blank screen of my computer and its blinking cursor. My mind was a torrent of blankness.

"Benj line 2." It was Noel looking at me as if something was wrong with my face.

"What?" I asked.

"Phone. Line 2." Noel said without looking at me as he returned to his desk.

I picked up the phone on my desk.

"Hello." It was Weng. I smiled.

"My love," I said.

"I left the house."

"Where are you?"

"All I have are the clothes in my luggage. I didn't take any of the stuff he bought for me."

"Where are you?"

"I'm calling from a pay phone outside the supermarket. I did it. I left him."

"What did he say? He knows?"

"Of course I told him. Then he said I should talk to you first. What does he mean?"

"He's trying to change my mind."

"How? Did you change your mind?"

"Never." I swallowed hard.

"So what did he tell you?"

"He says he'll give me the Amelia Earhart stuff."

"And what did you say?"

"I'll pick you up now."

"And then?"

"You'll move into my apartment."

"I don't want to live there."

"Temporary only. We'll look for another one."
"I'm craving. Green mangoes and fish sauce."
"I know where to get them."
"I think I'm happy."
"Let's not think at all."

85

AT the office on the following day, I saw an unmarked, brown shoe box on my desk. No one knew who put it there. I opened it and it was full of ashes. I was pretty sure that it was from *Tun* Jack—who else?—and it was his way of informing me that the ashes were the remains of the supposed photo of Amelia Earhart and whatever physical evidence he had of her supposed presence on Saipan. It could have been anyone in that photo, I told myself; and that jacket could have belonged to *Tun* Jack himself.

Manny said I should go ahead and write another feature story about the box of ashes. He gave me a call late Thursday evening, just before midnight. I was putting the front page to bed. He said it was 5 a.m. in Stockton, California. Where's Stockton, I asked. A five-hour drive from L.A., he said. He and his wife were working as caregivers at a nursing home owned by a Filipino-American.

"It's a shitty job," Manny said. "But my employer could get me a work visa and, eventually, a green card. My employer's OK. She's a friend of a relative." He wanted to know how things were with the newspaper and the island. So I told him.

"Keep writing about the Earhart stuff," he said.

"Other than a box of ashes, I got nothing."

"Write about it anyway. For the record."

"The wires won't pick it up."

"Maybe they won't, but get in touch with the Amelia groups in the states. Your friend Rob knows them, right?"

"My best friend."

Manny chuckled. "Move on."

"I know."

"How's Weng?"

"She wants to quit her job."

"Why?"

"The old man got her that job."

"So?"

"We'll find another job for her."

"Did he agree to a divorce?"

"Not yet."

"Hah."

"Yeah."

"Sweet?"

"Oh she's divorcing me. Rob, I think, is paying for her lawyer and the filing fee."

"Good man."

"Hah."

"You'll sign it?"

"I'll sign it over and over."

Manny chuckled. Before he hung up, he told me he'd write a novel about his experiences at the nursing home. "Or maybe a screenplay. Yeah. I'm banking on white liberal guilt." We laughed.

Our new reporter, Andy, arrived a few days later. He was in his early 20s. Single. Eager. He had been a features writer at one of the Manila dailies. He wanted to experience news writing, he said. He was into leftist politics—and poetry, and he wanted to discuss Mao's talks at the Yenan forum with me. I smiled at him as I mentally rolled my eyes. Andy and I had a lot of mutual acquaintances in Manila. Sam told me to take the newbie to Capital Hill, so I did. There I introduced him to the lawmakers who were in their offices. The usual suspects like Congressman Acosta and Senator Guzman, the reformists who were now the rah-rah boys of the governor and Senator Jimenez.

"Welcome to our island!"

"So you're the new guy!"

"About time. We're sick and tired of seeing Benjie here every day."

Laughter.

At the governor's office, Andy met the governor's spokesman, Jim, and the governor himself.

"I'll bet you're a way better reporter than this guy here," the governor told Andy, smiling, pointing at me.

"My kid," Jim said, "is a way better reporter than Benjie, and my kid is 3 years old."

More laughter.

"You guys do recall, of course, that I choose what news stories to run and I also write the editorials?" I said, grinning.

"That's why we love you!" Jim said. The governor chuckled. Andy looked amused.

The governor asked me, "Still searching for Amelia Earhart?"

"Aren't we all?" I replied.

ACKNOWLEDGEMENTS

In writing this novel, I consulted the following books about Amelia Earhart and/or her final flight:

Amelia Earhart: The Truth at Last
by Mike Campbell (Sunbury Press, Pennsylvania, 2016)

Amelia Earhart Lives
by Joe Klaas (McGraw Hill Book Co., New York, 1970)

The Sound of Wings: The Life of Amelia Earhart
by Mary S. Lovell (St. Martin's Griffin; New York, 1989)

Also helpful were the various online articles and blog sites about the famed pilot and her disappearance.

About the author

Zaldy Dandan studied broadcast journalism at the Polytechnic University of the Philippines in Manila, and wrote and/or edited for the *Philippine Daily Globe*, *Manila Standard* and *The Manila Times*. He is the former editor of *The Marianas Observer* and is the editor of *Marianas Variety*. He is the recipient of the Best Editorial Writer Award of the U.S. Society of Professional Journalists, and the Northern Marianas Humanities Award for Outstanding Contributions to Journalism. He has also been awarded fellowships to the University of the Philippines National Writers Workshop in Baguio City and the national writers workshop in Dumaguete City. His book of poems, *We'll Kiss Like It's Air and We're Running Out of It*, and short stories, *Die! Bert! Die*, are also available on amazon.com/. Since Oct. 23, 1993, he has been residing and working on Saipan, the Northern Marianas.

Made in the USA
Columbia, SC
04 January 2020

A young reporter from the Philippines, Benjie signed up for a newspaper job on the Pacific island of Saipan to earn more money. He expected a year or two of a profitable tropical vacation—not an eye-opening, mind-boggling, life-changing experience. It turns out that the small island, which played a big part in recent American history, may also hold the key to solving one of the 20th century's most enduring mysteries: Amelia Earhart's final flight in the summer of 1937.

Love, lust, politics, history—and a multi-ethnic cast of characters that include hucksters, visionaries, true believers and cynics. Did Benjie solve the mystery or uncover another one?

Zaldy Dandan is editor of *Marianas Variety*, Saipan's oldest newspaper. His book of poems, *We Will Kiss Like It's Air and We're Running Out of It*, and book of short stories, *Die! Bert! Die!*, are also available on amazon.com. He lives on the island with his wife, son, daughter and Bob the cat.